A SECRET ATTRACTION

"I've a great interest in angling," Wylde explained. "In fact, that interest is what prompted me to settle along the Dove River—that and my penchant to be alone."

Lissa glanced at him. "You prefer solitude, my lord?"

His dark gaze flickered. "Something akin to that."

Lissa moved forward, rounding the huge table spread with a veritable treasure of angling supplies. " 'Tis quite a collection."

"Is it?"

She nodded, letting out her breath over the sight of it all. "Indeed. There are feathers here that cannot be found along the Dove. And these hooks?" She reached for a particularly shiny silver one that was small and very fine. "They have been fashioned by a master craftsman."

"Continue," Wylde said, rounding the table to stand beside her.

Lissa looked up, taken aback by the sheer nearness of him, and by his deep, husky tone. His penetrating gaze, his voice, his closeness, and especially the masculine, clean scent of him were wreaking havoc with her insides. In fact, she didn't know how long she could manage to stand so near to him and act as though nothing was amiss with her heartbeat. Truth of the matter was, her heart was pounding a thrilling beat. The path her thoughts were taking was most unladylike, Lissa knew, but she couldn't help herself. Nor could she stop. She was very much affected by Lord Wylde. . . .

Books by Lindsay Randall

LADY LISSA'S LIAISON

MISS MEREDITH'S MARRIAGE

MISS MARCIE'S MISCHIEF

FORTUNE'S DESIRE

JADE TEMPTATION

DESIRE'S STORM

Published by Zebra Books

LADY LISSA'S LIAISON

Lindsay Randall

Zebra Books
Kensington Publishing Corp.

http://www.zebrabooks.com

ZEBRA BOOKS are published by

Kensington Publishing Corp.
850 Third Avenue
New York, NY 10022

First Printing: August, 1998
10 9 8 7 6 5 4 3 2 1

Printed in the United States of America

A NOTE FROM THE AUTHOR

I hope Regency readers enjoy this foray into the country-side of England's rich past. I wanted to write a Regency story not set amidst the drawing rooms of London, but rather one that captured the excitement of fly-fishing during its early stages, that illustrated the fervor with which the true anglers of this time went to the water, and one that also highlighted the passion of two characters who realized the gift of a river surrounded and inhabited by life and the beauty of God's vast bounty.

The idea for this book was born during several fly-fishing trips to the high mountain streams of Hunts Run in Cameron County, Pennsylvania, with my father and my son.

What a treasure to watch my father pass on his devotion of protecting and preserving nature to my son, and what a pleasure to sit quietly by a clear, tumbling brook and have my father tell me about the origins of fly-fishing, and of how many gentlemen in England's history found challenges and contentment alongside that country's rivers and streams.

My father learned to tie flies at the knee of an old mountain man, and was night fishing for trout long before it became popular. He was also crusading to preserve nature years before doing so became politically correct. A fly-fishing historian of sorts, and a definite defender of nature, it is my father's knowledge I've sprinkled throughout this tale of an angling lord and a spirited, nature-loving lady.

I would like to take this opportunity to thank him for sharing his vast collection of rare books on trout and angling, and for being so generous with his time and knowledge. I shall always remember the many hours we spent sitting at his kitchen table as he talked about the woods he loves so much—and I shall never forget his warning that life, as we know it, hinges on the preservation of our planet's precious water bodies. . . .

Lindsay Randall

Chapter 1

At the cusp of springtime and the Summer Season, along the gin-clear Dove River with its tumbling currents and clouds of mayflies flitting about, there appeared to be a happening in the making. A number of smart, sleek carriages could be viewed rumbling atop the rustic lanes of Derbyshire, each one led by the best of horseflesh and all commanded by the most notable and eligible gentlemen of London Town. Everyone was abuzz about the unexpected guests, and every local from miles around was wondering what—or perhaps *who*—had been the catalyst to bring so many titled swell into their midst.

They did not have to look far.

Her name was Lady Lissa Arianna Lovington, a comely female of the bluest blood, who had ended the mourning for her father only a fortnight prior and who was now heiress to a staggering sum of riches as well as the sprawling lands of Clivedon Manor in Derbyshire.

The lady's doting father had kept the beautiful Lissa far

from the fuss of the Metropolis, but word of her exceptional loveliness was a secret that could not be contained. With eyes as blue as a summer sky, her hair a glorious halo of shimmering blond, and her skin tinted with a perfect peaches-and-cream hue, Lady Lissa had blossomed into the vision of an angel, with a sweet disposition that was wont to rival the same. Following the unfortunate demise of her father, it had not taken long for a number of eligible gentlemen from Town to descend upon her quiet solitude and send missives her way, all of them eager to offer for her hand.

Soon, all of Derbyshire was agog with the news of Lady Lissa's many suitors. The local proprietors, innkeeps, ostlers and chambermaids were ecstatic due to the presence of the monied visitors. Maids and matrons were suddenly donning their most comely attire, while brothers, fathers and grandfathers alike were busy sharpening their card-playing and story-telling skills, intent on outwitting or, at the very least, amusing the unexpected guests.

The only one in Derbyshire *not* pleased by this invasion of suitors from the Metropolis was Lady Lissa herself. In fact, at the very unfashionable hour of dawn on a misty morn in early summer, Lissa was not asleep in her bed and dreaming visions of matrimony, but was instead in the hills of Derbyshire, on her hands and knees alongside the fog-covered river, groping for a cadis-worm casing in the cool waters of the Dove and hoping to extricate herself from this slew of suitors. Her satchel, filled with charcoals, paints, sketch pad and nature diary, lay beside her on the riverbank. She'd chosen a somewhat hidden spot near the river to spread her blanket, but one that gave her a good view of the riverbank tracing its way along each side of her.

"Heavens," said Lissa as she looked at a clump of wet reeds in her hand, "not a Cadis-worm in the bunch." She dropped the reeds, as big as the compass of a two-pence, back into the water, then thrust her hand in a second time.

"Truly, Tilly," she said to her young abigail seated beside her, "last year at this time I could pull out three or more with just one scoop of my palm. Perhaps this is not a good year for the insects. Perhaps there will be a small number of the Cadis that will actually fly. Perhaps ... *Tilly?* Are you listening to me?"

The young maid, with her mop of riotous red curls, jerked into motion, sitting up straight. "Oh, yes, m'lady. I be listenin'. And no, I canno' fly. O' course I canno' *fly*," Tilly said, trying very hard to look as though she was awake and had been listening to her lady's every word.

Lady Lissa frowned. "Tilly, you've fallen asleep."

The abigail blinked very green but sleepy eyes, failing miserably at appearing alert. "But it be so very early, m'lady," she whined.

Lissa sagaciously ignored the familiar, high-pitched sound. "Every angler, Tilly," Lissa pointed out, "knows that early morning is the best time to catch fish."

"But we *ain'* catchin' fish," Tilly moaned, rubbing the sleep from her eyes. "We be sittin' on the cold ground by a foggy river lookin' fer—oh, *la,* m'lady, could you please tell me again what we be lookin' fer?"

Lissa felt the undeniable urge to click her tongue in exasperation, but resisted the temptation. "We are not really looking for anything, Tilly," she explained patiently. "Rather, we are *waiting* for someone, but we do not want it to appear as *though* we are waiting. So we shall bide our time searching for worms, of which there should be a great many. There is the piper-cadis, and one called a cockspur, and there are straw worms, also known as ruff-coat, whose casing is made of little pieces of bents and waterweeds and condensed with slime and—"

"Ugh," said Tilly, a look of pure disgust crossing her features.

Lissa ignored it. A moment of silence stretched between them as Lissa turned once again to the task of searching for a cadis-worm in the river's water, her gaze surrepticiously turning now and then to glance down the water's edge, past the foliage behind which she'd positioned herself.

Tilly, her curiosity getting the best of her, plopped forward onto her hands and knees, staring down the length of the river alongside her lady. In a hushed whisper, she asked, "And who, m'lady, might we be waitin' *fer?*"

Lissa swished her hand through the tumbling currents of the river. "His name is Gabriel Gordon," she said, trying to keep her voice even. "He is the sixth Earl of Wylde, and—"

Tilly sucked in a sharp gasp, bolting upright.

"What?" Lissa exclaimed, startled. "Is something wrong? Are you ill?"

The abigail, eyes wide, clutched both hands over her heart in a dramatic fashion. "Lawks, m'lady, I not be the ill one, but you must surely be, forgive me fer sayin' so!"

"Tilly, whatever is the matter with you?"

"Oo, m'lady, that name you just uttered. Lord Thinga-mabob—"

"Lord Wylde?"

The abigail cringed as though Lissa had called up the devil himself. "Yes! Ooh, 'e's a bad 'un, 'e is. Terrible trouble. They call 'im the 'eartless One, they do, fer good reason. Tell me ye not be thinkin' of meetin' the likes of *'im.*"

Lissa stared up at her very flighty maid. In a firm tone, she said, "I am and I will. Now, do sit down and calm yourself. There is no reason for you to be so upset."

"No reason?" Tilly exclaimed, sitting as she was told to do, but fidgeting nonetheless. "Coo, m'lady, Lor' Wylde is known to be a—an *ogre,*" she gasped, drawing her hands from her chest only to wring them together in a nervous way. "Why, 'e's killed dozens of men an—and a wud-be bride t' boot'"

"Nonsense, Tilly. The man has never been charged with anything so reprehensible as murder. It is all nothing more than malicious gossip," said Lissa, then stopped herself.

She'd heard all of the rumors surrounding the enigmatic Lord Wylde. In fact, she'd spent the last few weeks studying his character, digging up every tidbit she could find about the man. There hadn't been much of recent note to unearth other than that he'd landed himself in Derbyshire and was known to have become a recluse, intent on spending his time fishing the waters of the Dove.

It was the stories of his previous life in London that interested Lissa and had propelled her to venture this morning onto the very lands that he haunted.

Thinking of those stories, Lissa looked at her abigail, and said, "I want you to calm down and listen to me, Tilly."

The maid, her green eyes as wide as full moons, clutched her hands together in an effort to still them. She took a deep breath. "I be listenin'," she said nervously.

"Good. Because what I am about to tell you is just between us, and you must never breathe a word of this to anyone."

"Me chaffer's mum, m'lady."

Lissa frowned, not always understanding Tilly's choice of words. "I hope it will be," she said, guessing that what her abigail was trying to say was that Lissa's secret was safe with her. Casting about her mind for a proper place to begin, Lissa said, "It is no secret to everyone in Derbyshire that a number of gentlemen from Town have come calling, each of them hoping to offer for my hand."

"No secret at all," said Tilly sincerely, "you be that beautiful, m'lady."

"Or that rich," muttered Lissa to herself.

"Whut's that, m'lady?"

"Nothing," said Lissa, shaking her head and continuing. "You see, Tilly, I have become overwhelmed by the many, er, uh, gentlemen who have suddenly invaded my life, not to mention my privacy, and who seem to believe that I should welcome their overeager courtship."

"Such as Lor' Langford?" Tilly asked, her green eyes suddenly going dreamy as she said the man's name. " 'E

be ever so handsome, Lor' Langford be. Oh, coo, m'lady,
'e even gave you 'is special pendant t' wear. I noticed that
right fast.''

Lissa instinctively touched the hand-painted locket the
blond-haired Lord Roderick Langford had given her just
the day before. He'd boldly looped it about her neck,
telling her that if she did not return it to him by the end
of the Summer Season, he would know she had accepted
his suit; whether or not she returned his locket was to be
a private sign to him.

Lissa wore the locket now not because she was interested
in the man, but because she had not been able to unfix
the drafted clasp and remove it from her neck. Had she
had a choice, she would have taken it off and sent it back
to him posthaste. But, alas, the clasp would not give, and
in her haste to be up before dawn this morning, she had
forgotten all about the locket and the too-handsome Langford as well.

Until now.

Tilly's mention brought to the forefront once again all
of Lissa's misgivings at finding herself a very rich heiress
who was now considered fair game by too many gentlemen.
She suspected Lord Langford's interest in her—and the
others from the Metropolis as well—was dictated more by
her rich purse than anything else.

Her doting father had left Lissa a very wealthy woman.
While alive, he had kept her protected from fortune hunt-
ers and those who would break her heart. He'd allowed her
to pursue her passions of painting, sketching and writing in
her nature journal. But now, the idyllic peace she'd once
known had been shattered by invitations, calling cards,
and a host of men like the golden-haired Lord Langford
who believed they could woo her with pretty words and
empty promises.

Lissa wanted them all gone from her life.

But how could one turn down so many with just a single sweep?
she'd wondered. And then a thought had come to her.

'Twas a dangerous thought. Perhaps a bit too risky. But it seemed a good enough plan.

Looking at Tilly, Lissa decided she would need to let one person in on her plot—even if that person was her flighty maid.

"Though Lord Langford has been nothing but polite in my presence," Lissa began, "I feel nothing for him, Tilly, and do not wish to encourage his suit. Nor do I wish to be bothered by any of the other gentlemen who have traveled here from London to meet with me. That is why we are now sitting alongside the river and looking for Cadis-worm casings while waiting for Lord Wylde."

The abigail puckered her freckled brow. "La, m'lady, but I be confused," Tilly said, exasperated and very worried. "The 'eartless Lor' Wylde be a dangerous sort o' fellow. Not at all whut yer father wud 'ave wanted you t' be near. Why, 'e be a bride murderer!"

"Hush, Tilly," Lissa said firmly. "The woman wasn't his bride, but his would-be bride. And, regardless, the entire story of his part in the woman's demise is merely a rumor unproved."

"Not accordin' to whut I hears below stairs, m'lady," warned Tilly in her usual breach of decorum, "and whut 'bout all them duels 'e fought? No rumors there."

"You are quite right about the latter," Lissa acknowledged, to which her abigail sucked in another gasp. "But," Lissa went on, not pausing, "his lordship's famous, er, rather, infamous, past is precisely the reason I seek him out today. You see, I have decided that I need to affix my name to a man who is both a threat and a danger to the many gentlemen who have come calling for my hand. Once they learn that I have been in the company of someone so—so unacceptable as his lordship, they will undoubtedly withdraw, and I will be left alone, able to live my life as I see fit and not be bothered by their presence. It is, I believe, the only thing left for me to do since none of them have yet taken note of the fact that I wish not to be wooed or married at this time."

Her abigail appeared quite dumbfounded and for once speechless.

"Tilly," said Lissa, "did you hear what I said?"

"Lawks, m'lady, I 'eard, but I not be believin' it."

Lissa sat back and pulled a small handkerchief from the inner pocket of her pretty skirt, wiping the wetness of the river from her hands. "It is not so unbelievable," she insisted. "Indeed, I think it is a truly famous idea."

"But Lor' Wylde is . . . is—"

"Not to be trusted," Lissa supplied. "I know. I have heard the same. I've also heard he is a terror with both sword and pistol, can outride, outshoot and outmaneuver any of his previous peers. And," she said lastly, "I know that he is considered a black sheep among the *ton*. He has become an outcast due to his many unseemly actions and his supposed part in a certain woman's death. He is purportedly a powder keg, smoldering to go off at any moment. He is frightening and frightful and a terrible scourge on good Society."

Tilly bobbed her head at all of these descriptions.

"Even so," Lissa went on, *"he* is the one I've chosen with whom to align my good name. And so here we are, awaiting his arrival along the river's edge. He is known to have taken up fly angling for trout in Derbyshire. Some say it is the balm for his black heart, while others say he simply enjoys slicing open the neck of anything alive."

Tilly looked perfectly aghast. "And whut if, m'lady, the neck 'e be wantin' t' slice be yer own?" she whispered.

"What a ridiculous possibility," Lissa admonished.

Tilly obviously did not think it so ridiculous. Trying another bent, the maid said, "Well then, whut if 'is lordship takes a keen likin' to *you?* Whut then, m'lady?"

Lissa paused, taken aback by the question, but then quickly shook her head. "Another absurd notion, Tilly," she assured her maid. "I am not at all the type of female he would be interested in. I merely wish to make his acquaintance and be seen in his presence a time or two. Nothing more."

"Yer father wud not be 'appy knowin' o' yer plan," Tilly warned.

"My father," Lissa answered, feeling a deep twinge in her heart at the mentioning of the one person she'd loved above any and all things, "would want *me* to do what is best for *me.*"

"And yer aunt?" Tilly dared to ask.

Lissa wrinkled her nose. Aunt Prudence wouldn't like it at all, she knew. Though Aunt Pru had been a sweet dear by helping Lissa through the loss of her father, Lissa secretly could not wait for the woman to take her leave. She was making noises about Lissa going to Town for a formal come out. Only the fact that Lissa had still been in mourning saved her from having to make an entrance into Society this past spring. Her father had spared her from the ordeal the previous years. He'd known very well Lissa had no interest in being placed on the Marriage Mart, and he'd been loath to tear her away from her beloved Derbyshire.

"Aunt Prudence will also want what is best for me," Lissa insisted.

"And the 'eartless Lor' Wylde be that?"

"Yes," said Lissa, resolve in her tone, "he is."

Of a sudden, there came a slight sound from somewhere behind and beyond them.

Tilly, nervous as a young filly, bounded to her feet. "Oh, la, m'lady, do not make me stay and meet the ogre!" she cried.

"Hush," scolded Lissa, hoping his lordship wouldn't be turned away by the sounds of their voices. "Heavens, Tilly, I've been plotting this meeting for weeks. I do not wish for the sound of your voice to scare him off. Now, do sit down and act as though the two of us are simply here by chance. Hand me my sketchbook, will you?"

Tilly thrust her hands into her lady's satchel, pulling out not only the sketchbook, but a number of charcoals as well, paints and even Lissa's nature journal, spilling everything onto the ground. "La, I be nervous," she gasped.

"Calm yourself, Tilly," Lissa instructed, feeling her own heart beginning to pound. She heard no more sounds of anyone coming toward the river. Perhaps what they had heard had been some woodland animal, or maybe a shift in the wind. Or perhaps the reclusive Lord Wylde had become aware of their presence and decided to leave.

Lissa hoped the latter wasn't the case. She tried to relax; but her own nerves were suddenly frayed, and she questioned her foolish choice of toying with and making use of a man so dangerous as Gabriel Gordon, the sixth Earl of Wylde.

Positioning her sketchbook firmly upon her lap, she turned her face toward the moving waters of the Dove with its limestone bed and then took up a piece of charcoal. She tried to sketch what she saw, tried in vain to capture the precise lines of the early morn, with the fog hovering above the water, the dawn's clear light slipping and slanting through the foliage, but her thoughts were far too scattered for her to concentrate. Instead, she managed only to scribble a to-do list, which wasn't a "list" at all, but only included the initials G.G. and the words *must meet*.

Tilly, like a nervous animal about to spring forth, hovered near her on the blanket. "I—I fear I'm goin' t' wet meself," whispered the abigail.

Lissa shushed the girl, her own insides aquiver.

A ways down the river's edge there came a rustling of movement. Both Tilly and Lissa looked up as a man walked into view.

Tilly immediately gulped in a frightened gasp of air.

Lissa, however, let out a satisfied sigh. *He is perfect for my plan,* she thought, instantly pleased by the deliciously dominating figure of the man.

Tall, unutterably and darkly handsome, with a body that

seemed hewn from sturdy oak, he moved forward with a grace known only to the woodland animals Lissa so loved to sketch. He walked very quietly, with reverence to the fish in the water no doubt, and carried with him an angling rod and a long-handled net. Strapped about his muscled chest was a wicker basket. His hair was jet black, longish, marvelously shagged. His shoulders were very broad, and his eyes, when the morning light reflected in them off the water, Lissa noted, were as black as a funeral shroud.

Tilly jumped up. "Eeek!" she gasped. "He be death come to life! He be—"

"Enough," Lissa said in a fast whisper. But Tilly was already running for the safety of the trees, leaving her lady behind. Lissa ground her back teeth together. So much for having her maid as chaperone.

Determined to go through with her plan in spite of her abigail's weak constitution, Lissa steeled her resolve. She needed a way of thwarting her suitors as a whole, and linking her good name with that of the maligned Lord Wylde would certainly do the trick. None of those popinjays would dare venture where they believed the dangerous Lord Wylde trod. They would all tuck their tails and run back to the Metropolis once Lissa made everyone in Derbyshire believe she had promised herself to his lordship. All she need do was create the illusion of a liaison between the two of them, and her problem would be solved.

Doing so, of course, would take time—not to mention a bold bit of deceit. She glanced once again toward the man so many had labeled "heartless." He stood with his feet apart, his black gaze on the river, one strong and very capable hand wrapped about his fishing rod, his other fist clutching his long-handled net. He appeared as though he were deeply studying some challenge he would like to turn inside out and upside down. He looked downright fierce, in fact.

Lissa felt a gnawing of hesitancy beginning deep inside her as she noted that his mouth was hardened and that it only served to accent the stubborn jut of his chin. Heavens, was there nothing soft about the man she'd chosen to aid her cause?

Before she fled from the scene as Tilly had already done, she forced herself to calm down. Affixing a bright smile to her face, Lissa called a cheery "Hullo!" then waved to the man as she rose to her feet and stepped out from behind the foliage she'd chosen to position herself alongside.

His gaze ripped toward her as though she had fired a gun. He did not smile, did not wave.

No matter. Lissa kept moving, her prettiest smile plastered on her face.

"Good morning," she called, drawing near and noticing that his lordship's eyes were a great deal blacker than she'd first thought. They were also cold and chilling, devoid of any warmth. And he was taller, too—if that were possible—than he'd seemed from afar. She felt immediately daunted by his presence, and by the fact he clearly did not appreciate *her* presence in what he obviously deemed as *his* domain.

"I see you have come afishing, sir. And what a fine morning to do so." Lissa kept her voice light and breezy, hoping to set the tone for their conversation.

"Fine?" he muttered darkly. "Hardly that. The fog is lifting early. The trout will become skittish with the morning's light. They do not like to be disturbed."

Like the trout he'd come to find, Lissa guessed that the Heartless Lord Wylde did not like to be disturbed either. Still, she kept up her cheery facade, refusing to back down or to be intimidated in any way. "So you are an angler, are you, sir?"

His right hand tightened about his angling rod with a death grip. "An obvious fact," he said.

Lissa felt foolish and suddenly dry-mouthed, but rushed on. "I believe your estate marches with mine on this side of the Dove, sir."

"Does it?"

She nodded.

"And you are?"

"Lady Lissa Lovington of Clivedon Manor. I am—"

"Up early," he cut in. "Does every lady in Derbyshire rise with the sun and walk along the river?"

Lissa blinked. "No . . . at least, I do not believe so."

"Good," he muttered.

Lissa quelled a frown. He was not the easiest of persons with whom to speak. Forcing her smile not to waver, she said, "I believe you are Lord Wylde, are you not?"

"Aye," came his growl of an answer.

So much for a warm greeting, she thought. Lissa nodded toward her blanket that lay beyond the clump of foliage. "I often come to the river's edge at this time to sketch, my lord. The light is best at dawn. Crisp and clear."

He said nothing.

Lissa knew then that was his cue for her to leave him to his angling, but she wasn't about to leave. Not now. Not when she'd ventured this far.

"You would not mind if I linger here to sketch while you fish, would you?" she asked.

He arched one dark brow, looking past her to her blanket scattered with her sketchbook, charcoals, paints and journal, then glanced back at her. "You may do whatever you wish, my lady."

Lissa instantly brightened. Perhaps this chance meeting would not turn out so horribly after all, she thought. With an engaging smile sent his way, she turned and headed back toward her blanket. Once there, she glanced his way again, and then set herself to the task of sketching the view of the river in earnest. Talking to him at length could come later, she told herself. For now, she decided, she must form some unspoken bond between them, and what better way to do so than for the two of them to go about their endeavors within short reach of each other?

Lissa had no sooner scratched out the words *G.G.—must*

meet and outlined her sketch than his lordship moved past behind her and headed upriver, his angling pole positioned over one broad shoulder.

"*Oh,*" she murmured, in spite of herself, "you—you are leaving already, sir?" she called. "Why, you haven't even touched the tip of your pole to the water."

"And do not intend to," he said, not looking back.

"But I thought—er, rather, it *seemed*—you would fish here," Lissa said, hoping she didn't sound as desperate as she felt.

He reluctantly paused to glance over one shoulder, studying her for a fraction of a moment. "You thought wrong, my lady," he said, and then, with nary a by-your-leave, he headed away from her.

Lissa, mouth agape, watched him go.

"Lawks, m'lady," whispered a voice from the thicket behind her, "did I no' tell you he be a ogre?"

Lissa jerked her head toward the sound of Tilly's voice. "A lot of help you've been," Lissa said, thoroughly disgusted with the turn of events. "I thought you'd gone back to the house."

"Oh, I wanted t' do just that, m'lady, but I be thinkin' you may be needin' me so I stayed." There came a rustle of leaves as Tilly speared several vines apart with her fingers and peeked through them. Her green eyes were large in the wreath of foliage. "You still be fixin' t' spend time w' 'is lordship, m'lady?" she asked, voice quivering.

Lissa glanced in the direction Lord Wylde had taken. "Most definitely. His presence, and his alone, will assure me of ending all the unwanted advances that have come my way."

"But 'e be nowheres near present," the maid pointed out.

Lissa frowned. "A mere inconvenience at the moment, Tilly." Her gaze darkened as she added, "I never truly believed his lordship and I would have anything in common. From what I've gleaned of his character, the two of us are as different as night and day. No, Tilly, what I envisioned is merely the *illusion* of a liaison with the dangerous Lord Wylde.''

"A *whut?*"

"A liaison. I want only for all the eligible gentlemen in Derbyshire to *think* that his lordship and I are . . . involved. The man can stare daggers at me and it will make no difference. I really do not give a whit for what he thinks of me. I wish only that others believe his interest of me is keen. Now, are you going to come out of the bushes and join me, or must I go this alone?''

"Coo, m'lady, but I be afeared! I—''

"Never mind,'' said Lissa abruptly, releasing her abigail of any intuitive urge to protect her "You may stay where you are. I shall return for you.''

"But I—''

"You heard me, Tilly.''

Lissa quickly snatched up her satchel, shoved her charcoals, paints, sketchbook and journal into it, and leaving her blanket behind, hastened after Lord Wylde.

Tilly, bounding out of the thicket a few moments later, wrung her hands together.

"Oh, me,'' she fretted, debating whether or not to follow her lady's footsteps. Going back to the house, though, seemed a saner and far safer decision.

Besides, if her lady wished to have her good name maligned with Lord Wylde's, what better way to do so than by the many servants of Clivedon Manor to hear the tale firsthand from Tilly's own lips? By sundown, everyone in Derbyshire, via the gossip vine of the servants, would know of her lady's "liaison'' with the wicked Lord Wylde. It seemed a clever plan, and one that would assure that her lady would not need to step one foot near the nasty Lord Wylde ever again after today.

Having a strong purpose at last, Tilly raced back for the house.

Chapter 2

Gabriel Gordon, the sixth Earl of Wylde, felt for the first time in a good many years as though the breath had been knocked out of him.

He didn't like the feeling. Not at all.

He'd come to the river's edge as he'd always done these past few weeks in search of solitude, and certainly not to be bothered by a female with eyes the color of wild English bluebells, a smile so dazzling it outlit the sun, and blond ringlets so pure in color that they seemed a nimbus about her heart-shaped and very lovely face.

That she reminded him sharply of another woman—one from long ago in his past—did not seem to matter as much to him at the moment as did the fact of what the mere sight of her made him feel: edgy, interested, and very much aware that she was a female and he was a male.

Amazing! In just the flash of a few moments the woman had made him experience emotions he'd kept buried for years.

Not about to fish the waters where she lingered, Gabriel made haste to move upriver, to a favored trout hole where one especially elusive trout had outfoxed him for many days. He'd made a promise to himself that he would hook the fish by summer's end . . . and for Wylde, a promise made was a promise kept.

He dropped his wicker basket onto the ground, flipped open the lid, and studied the assortment of handmade flies impaled on the inside cushion of sheepskin affixed to the upper lid.

He glanced once at the river, his black eyes narrowing somewhat as he attempted to decide which fly would be best. Trout were very persnickety, and a wrong fly chosen could end in disappointment for an angler. But though he tried to make a study of the various live flies hovering above the water and lingering near the banks and sides of the river, he saw only in his mind's eye a very beauteous face, pearl white teeth, a piquant rosebud of a mouth, and a halo of golden hair.

"Faith," Gabriel muttered to himself. He ripped off the hand-tied fly nearest to him. That done, he removed a silk worm gut leader from his soak box, glad to see that the silk was soft and pliable. He affixed the hook of the fly to this leader, then moved with hard purpose toward the water, angry with himself for being so haunted by a mere slip of a woman he'd happened to meet this day.

She was of no consequence, he told himself sternly. He would not see her again, of that he would make certain. His self-imposed exile amid the wilds of Derbyshire was intended to be just that; an exile, a place of perfect solitude, no interference and no chance meetings, no friends, no visitors, no nothing. That was how he wanted it. That, in fact, was how it *had* to be.

With the flick of one strong wrist, Gabriel cast the silk line, hearing the swish of it smooth out over the water. Beneath the surface of the water could be seen a good many trout bellying up near the silt-covered limestone bottom of the Dove. Gabriel gently hand-retrieved the line, pulling the silk back with his fingers and drawing the man-made fly through the water, hoping to illicit a bite from the hungry trout below. For all of his expert casting, though, he got nary a nibble.

Frowning, he flicked the pole, lifted the line, drew it in, then cast again on another spot upstream. Again, there came no bite.

It was then Gabriel noticed he was not alone.

He felt the presence of another. Felt it as surely as he did the pull of the current on his line, the feel of the moist and lifting fog on his skin, and the shimmer of a growing sun on his face. He turned his head ever so slightly.

There. Hidden behind the trees, among the foliage, a bright, effervescent light seemed to glow . . . it was *her*.

Damnation! Now why, he wondered, would a lady be up and about with the dawn, trailing after him alongside the foggy river? No doubt her purpose was a nefarious one. Such was the way of women; he alone knew that to be the truest of truths.

Gabriel finished his cast, drew his angling rod back, and cast again, no longer paying attention to the trout in the water. Suddenly, he had other things on his mind, not the least of which was a lady with a too-bright smile who had the power to cast him back into a past better left forgotten. . . .

Lissa finally caught up to Lord Wylde's long strides, finding that he'd chosen a narrow bend in the river where a huge, thick and rotting log had fallen across the water. She held back as he casted—of all choices—an artificial nymph, and wondered whether or not he knew of her presence. She decided that he must. Her father, an accomplished angler, had taught her that every man who ventures to the brook is aware of any and all things surrounding him. Surely the Heartless Lord Wylde knew of her presence. How rude of him not to acknowledge it.

Then again, she thought, it was highly rude of *her* to be following him so closely. But a decision made was a decision made, and Lissa had made a decision on which her precious freedom hinged.

She sturdied herself, took a deep breath, then stepped out of the foliage she'd been hiding behind, moving to the water's edge.

"Lord Wylde?" she called.

"Hellfire."

"Excuse me?" Lissa instantly stilled, pausing where she stood near the water.

"Your dress," said Gabriel Gordon, scowling, "is far too bright, Lady Lovington. You have frightened the trout."

"I hardly think that the color of my gown—" she began, but he wasn't listening.

With quick jerks of his powerful hands he reeled his line in, yanked his pole back over one shoulder, picked up his wicker basket and net, and then nimbly jumped atop the rotten log spanning the narrow length of water, easily picking his way to the opposite bank.

Lissa, feeling assaulted and wondering how she had piqued the man's ire by something so simple as the color of her gown, lifted her skirts with one hand and boldly proceeded after him.

"My lord?" she called, her feet, in her half boots, dangerously slipping once, twice and a third time atop the mossy log as she hastened after him.

He paused, now standing on the opposite riverbank, his gaze narrowing as he watched her weave her way precariously over the log. "Is there a reason you are following me?"

Lissa, her arms spread like the wings of a falcon in flight, tilted dangerously to the right, the weight of her satchel tugging her to one side. "Yes . . . I—I mean no . . . er, well . . . possibly," she answered, trying desperately to stay upright.

Gabriel folded his arms about his chest, his angling rod resting easily in the crook of one arm, his fishing net now dangling from a loop at his side. "Which is it, Lady Lovington?" he asked, impatience evident in his tone.

Oh dear, Lissa thought. She was making a muddle of things. Problem was, she hadn't intended to actually chase after him; but when he'd headed across the river, she'd thought she'd lose sight of him, and so like a perfect ninny she'd jumped atop the log and thought to follow suit.

Now, however, she was feeling an age-old sensation of nauseating vertigo. She'd first felt this sense of imbalance when she'd climbed atop a pony for the first—and last—time of her life many years ago. Since then, she'd learned to stay away from horses, not to mention high places.

She suddenly felt a roaring in her ears, as though a huge gust of wind had appeared, surrounding her. Felt, in fact, as though she might faint.

"Oh my," Lissa gasped. Very carefully, she moved her gaze to the Heartless Lord Wylde, who seemed utterly impervious to her plight. She debated whether or not to ask for his assistance as this wasn't at all turning out to be the encounter she'd planned with him. What must he think of her? What must he. . . .

Lissa felt a wave of nausea overcome her. "Lord Wylde," she gulped, "if you would be so kind, I, uh—"

"Bother it all," she heard him mutter.

Lissa cringed and closed her eyes, thinking she'd thoroughly undone their "chance" meeting, and just as quickly worried about whether or not she would fall into the water or just become violently ill.

Either way, she was doomed to a most embarassing fate.

To her surprise, Lord Wylde dropped the wicker basket from his shoulder, set down his net, and was, in a matter of a few agile strides, standing alongside her atop the downed log, his precious angling pole still held tight in one fist.

"Why the deuce did you climb atop this tree?" he demanded.

Lissa, eyes still closed, shook her head. "Foolishness perhaps?"

"No doubt," he answered.

It was then Lissa felt strong, warm and very large hands take hold of her shoulders. She felt Lord Wylde's fingers splay open and curl slightly over her. She was suddenly anchored safely atop the log, held securely in his very able grip.

Only then did Lissa feel safe enough to open her eyes. The first thing she viewed was his lordship's mouth, perfectly perfect in form, a very sensuous mouth indeed— one that had perhaps not smiled often enough . . . and was not smiling now.

Lissa's lashes quickly fluttered upward.

Not only was his mouth perfect, but his cheekbones as well; they were broad and flat and slightly tanned. And his eyes. Heavens, but his eyes were the most intriguing eyes she'd ever beheld. Dark. Fathomless. Heart-stoppingly deep and engaging.

Lissa felt herself beginning to swoon again, though this particular sensation had nothing to do with her vertigo.

"You're not going to be ill, are you?" he demanded, his fingers tightening about her, his angling rod now tucked into the crook of arm.

"No. I—I am quite all right," Lissa lied.

"The devil you are. You are pale and quivering."

"I shall be fine. Truly."

"Those half boots you are wearing are hardly the thing for traversing rotting logs. And that dress—"

"Is far too bright," she finished. "You've already mentioned that fact, Lord Wylde."

His splendid mouth formed a frown. "And have I mentioned that you are interfering in my angling?"

Lissa tried to smile. "No, but I gathered as much. Truly, sir, that was not my intent."

"What *was* your intent, pray tell, Lady Lovington?"

It was Lissa's turn to frown. She averted her gaze from

his, focusing instead on his fishing pole and the man-made fly tethered to the end of his line.

"I, uh, wished to talk about your angling for trout. Yes. That is it. That is the whole of it," she said, pleased with her quick thinking and rather relieved at the sight of the pathetically lacking nymph he had trussed to the end of his line.

"Oh?" Obviously, he did not believe her.

"Yes, of course. What else?" Lissa said, finding herself calm enough to paint yet another too-bright smile upon her lips. Insects were her specialty—and the insect Lord Wylde had chosen for his line was the most inappropriate, not to mention poorly tied, thing she had ever viewed. Assured of the fact that she knew of what she spoke, she said, "You see, sir, I have grown up alongside the Dove, and my father was an angler much like yourself. He taught me everything there is to know about the insects of this area."

"And?"

"And, well, you appear to be going about this all wrong, Lord Wylde."

"Going about *what* all wrong," he demanded. "Saving you from a dunk in the water? From what I see, you are not yet wet. Given another few moments to your own devices, you would have been thoroughly soaked."

Lissa felt duly chastised, but ignored her own embarrassment. "Besides that, my lord," she managed to say.

"What the devil are you talking about?"

"Your angling tactics, sir."

"What *about* them?" he bristled.

Lissa knew better than to correct a man about his angling. She knew that fishing was a very male type of endeavor, one that was wrapped up in all sorts of male pride and whatnot. But despite that fact, she couldn't help but make use of this most opportune moment. "I could not help but notice the fly you chose to cast," she said.

"You couldn't, could you?"

"Your choice is all wrong, my lord. At this time of year, you should be using a full-bodied fly and not a nymph."

Lord Wylde looked as though he'd swallowed one of those flies. "You actually know about nymphs and flies?"

Lissa bristled at his surprised tone, suddenly impervious to her still-precarious position atop the log. "Of course I do. I know insects, my lord. A green-drake would have been your best choice. Or perhaps a camlet fly. I've studied and sketched the insects of this area for as long as I can recall. I know, in fact, that an angler would be better served by a—"

Lissa suddenly let out an unintentional *oof* as her boots slid on the slippery log and she careened to one side. She instinctively reached one hand to her breast in a moment of fright, catching in her palm the hand-painted locket Lord Langford had given to her. The chain—blastedly too secure until now—burst apart.

Lissa gasped loudly as the troublesome locket fell free of her neck, falling down into the water. A huge, dark-colored river trout suddenly shot out from beneath the log and swallowed the locket whole, then just as quickly snapped back under the log.

"Oh my!" Lissa cried.

"What?" Lord Wylde demanded, her cry clearly setting the fear of the heavens into him. "What the duece is wrong now?" he groused, looping one strong arm about her tiny waist. "You're not going to fall. I've got you. Don't scream like that."

"The locket," Lissa gasped, very aware of his strong, muscular arm pinioning her to him, of the musky, masculine smell of his body, of the hard feel of his chest against hers.

Pressed against him, Lissa could sense the steady, deep rhythm of his heart, could feel her own heart pounding like the fast wings of a bird in flight. She hadn't expected to be so *affected* by the man.

Lissa glanced down, seeing his strong fingers splayed

about the curve of her waist. Such a large hand. And so warm, even through layers of fabric.

Staring up at him through her lashes, Lissa realized that he, too, seemed momentarily taken aback by the close contact of their bodies.

She had to shake her head to clear her thoughts. "Th—that trout ate my locket, my lord. Did you see? He just gulped it down!"

"I saw," he answered, voice husky, his gaze infinitely dark. He stared at her hard—as though surprised by what he saw, or perhaps, at what he was feeling inside of himself. " 'Tis gone now, you can be assured of that." He released his hold by slow degrees, his open palm skimming the small of her back as he slid his arm away from her.

A deep quiver of feeling pumped through Lissa. Again, she had to shake her head, had to force herself to remain focused on her purpose. "No, it—it cannot be. I—I *must* retrieve that locket."

"Was it a part of the family jewels?"

"No, of course not."

"Priceless, perhaps?"

"I—I do not believe so."

"Then forget about it," said Lord Wylde. Without another word, he took hold of her right hand and nimbly led her across to the side of the river, firmly planting her down onto the bank. Lissa was once again unnerved by the feel of his hands on her as he set her down.

"Do not look so Friday-faced," he growled. "You can purchase another locket."

"I cannot!" Lissa insisted, feeling miserable and turning to stare at the water where the trout made its home. "It is irreplaceable. It is . . . oh, drat, it is imperative I retreive *that* particular locket."

" 'Twould be a neat trick," he said, moving away from her to gather up his fishing basket and net. He looped the leather straps of both over his neck, tipped his angling pole over one shoulder, then glanced at her one more time before he took his leave. "The inner digestive juices of a trout are very powerful, Lady Lovington—or so I've learned. Within twenty-four hours, I suspect that locket will begin to disintegrate, unless it is made of gold."

"Gold?" Lissa paused, trying hard to remember from what exactly Lord Langford's locket had been fashioned. She hadn't a clue. She'd never wanted the blasted thing to begin with, and she'd certainly not spent an innordinate amount of time looking at or even touching the thing. "Truth to tell, sir, I—I am not certain *what* it was made of. I do know, though, that it was hand-painted. Yes, I am quite certain it was hand-painted."

He appeared a bit agitated by her vague description of a locket she seemed so bent on retrieving. His frown deepened. "Take my advice and forget about it, my lady." With that, he turned.

"Wait!" Lissa cried. "You—you are taking your leave? Just like that?"

He glanced over one shoulder, his darkling eyes narrowing. "And just what, alas, would you have me do?"

"Hook that trout, of course!"

Lord Wylde looked at her as though she'd sprouted two heads. And then he laughed.

The sound of his laughter smarted. "You find my situation amusing, sir?"

"I find you demanding a tall order, my lady."

"Not so tall," she insisted. "You've a pole in your hand, and you came here to fish. All you need do is fish for *that* particular trout."

He said nothing for a full minute, time in which Lissa feared she'd pushed his patience too far.

"I suggest you go home, Lady Lovington," he finally said, his words clipped, "and forget about your locket. No one will be catching that trout, not today anyway. He won't bite again for a good long while, trust me. I have been tracking him for a number of days, and this is the first I've seen him take a bite of anything."

With that, the Earl of Wylde headed away from her.

Lissa blew out an exasperated breath. Feeling desperate, she called after him: "The trout may bite if the right fly is placed before him, sir! He certainly will not surface for a nymph—or even for *any* of the other flies you have tied, if indeed their craftsmanship is anything like that sorrowful fly I viewed at the end of your line!"

Her words got his attention.

Wylde stopped and turned toward her, his gaze blacker than the darkest of crypts. *"Sorrowful?"*

Lissa gulped down a lump of fear in her throat.

"You heard me aright," she said, straightening, refusing to back down. "For all of your expert casting, sir, you obviously haven't a clue as to what type of fly should be affixed to your line."

"B'god, were you a man to say such a thing to me, I would—"

"You would *what?*" Lissa dangerously cut in. "Challenge me? Come now, Lord Wylde, you obviously have a hankering to catch some trout, and you just as obviously haven't the knowledge as to what bait to use. I can help you." She paused, then went on quickly, "And you—you can help *me.*"

One black brow lifted above his deep, dark eyes. "Oh? How so?"

"I—I can teach you about the insects that flit in the air above the Dove . . . and you, sir, can use that knowledge to hook the very trout that ate my locket and has thus far eluded your line."

Before she knew what he was about, Lord Wylde closed the distance between them, dropped his wicker basket and fine net to the ground near her feet, then kicked open the lid of the basket with one booted toe.

"Tell me," he demanded, "what fly of mine you think I should use to catch that wily trout."

Lissa blinked, her nerves frayed by his brusque tone and slamming about. "Well, I—"

"Tell me."

Lissa took in a steadying breath, licked her suddenly dry lips, and then glanced down at the basket. She frowned. It was just as she thought; every fly pinned to the snowy sheepskin was as flawed and pathetic as the nymph at the end of his pole.

She quirked one brow up at him. "The truth, sir?"

"Let's have it," he all but growled.

"Very well, but do remember that you insisted. The fact of the matter is, sir, none of them are a good choice. The tails are all too long, the bodies poorly made, and the hooks—"

"Faith," he muttered, slamming the lid shut once again. "That's enough."

Lissa cringed, fearing he was about to give her a scathing set-down. Clearly, he hadn't earned the title of heartless for no reason.

"Sir?" she managed, her voice sounding far too uncertain even to her own ears.

But Lord Wylde wasn't listening, nor was he even looking at her. He was looking at the river, and suddenly he was pacing, back and forth, his pole gripped in one hand, as with the other hand he raked his fingers through the black, shagged lengths of his hair. He appeared to be wrestling with some inner demon; looked frightfully agitated, in fact.

Lissa caught her bottom lip between her teeth, suddenly amazed at the fact that she was standing alone in the woods with a man so many deemed to be a dangerous cannon, a veritable devil come to walk the earth. That she'd insulted him with her assessment of his fly-tying skills was obvious. That she hadn't yet been cut down by his legendary fury was nothing short of remarkable.

She was debating whether to run for safety when he stopped pacing and abruptly turned toward her.

"Name it," he demanded suddenly.

Lissa, her nerves in a jumble, jerked to attention. "My lord?"

"The fly, my lady. Tell me what fly I should use at this time of year."

Lissa wondered if she heard him aright. "Does this mean that you will help—"

"Aye," he growled. "I will help, but mind you I cannot promise to do the impossible. The trout you wish to hook is an old and very cautious one. He hasn't grown huge for no reason. Only the smartest and most cautious trout know when to bite and when not to bite."

"Of—of course," said Lissa, feeling a bit of hope spring forth in her.

"As for your end of our bargain," Wylde continued, just as gruffly, "you will share with me your knowledge of insects."

"Oh, I will. I shall! In fact, I've my sketchbook with me. I've sketched all mannner of insects, sir. In great detail."

Lissa dove one hand into her satchel, producing her sketchbook and nature journal as well. "Come," she said, placing both atop the ground, "and see for yourself." She flipped a few pages into the journal, finding an entry she'd written about the green-drake fly. She opened her sketchbook to the exact spot where she'd created a watercolor of the insect. "Notice the tail, my lord. It is long, but not overly so. You want the trout to reach for the tail but to actually swallow the body with the hook. If the tail is too long, the trout will get a short strike, and you will have enticed him but not hooked him. And the body . . . can you see how it is nicely rounded? You must do the same with your handmade fly, but you must make certain that it won't unravel when the trout's strong jaw wraps about it."

She glanced up at him, seeing that he was very carefully studying her watercolor creation. "I—I can teach you how to tie such a fly, Lord Wylde." She frowned as she thought of the trout in the water, its belly filled with Lord Langford's locket—a locket that was disintegrating as they spoke. "We haven't much time, though, I am afraid."

Lord Wylde's black eyes met her blue ones. "You are thinking of your locket."

Lissa nodded.

He frowned, studied her, frowned some more.

"It must mean a great deal to you," he said at last.

Lissa thought of Lord Langford. She nodded. "Oh, yes," she breathed. *That blasted locket meant her freedom from at least one of her suitors.* "It is imperative that I get it back, sir."

Wylde debated some more. He clearly did not like the idea of striking a bargain with her, but at the same time he obviously desired to know all Lissa knew of insects.

Finally, he groused, "Then it appears, Lady Lovington, the two of us have a great deal of work to do."

Lissa wanted to smile with gratitude, but decided against it. Instead, she simply said, "Yes, that does seem to be the size of it, sir."

Chapter 3

Tilly broke free of the coppice and raced for the lawns of Clivedon Manor, nearly out of breath as she came upon Mrs. Rachett, who was busy hanging laundered linens on the line. The older woman barely glanced in Tilly's direction.

"Are you no' wonderin' whut I be about?" Tilly asked between huge, dramatic gulps of air.

"No," said Mrs. Rachett, spreading a fine, white table cloth onto the line. She proceeded to beat the wrinkles out of the linen with her plump, raw-boned hands.

Tilly decided she might just as well rush into the words she'd been rehearsing during her mad dash back to Clivedon Manor. "Oh, la," she said to the disinterested housekeeper, "I be thinkin' surely *you* of all those in m'lady's keep wud be wonderin' 'bout 'er doin's."

The stern-faced Mrs. Rachett pursed her wrinkled lips, not replying.

Tilly decided to cut to the heart of it all. "M'lady is in the woods with the 'eartless Lord Wylde, she is, and glad about 'at fact! Wants t' spend 'er day wi' 'im, she does, and wants no' a word of 'er lee-a . . .'' Tilly stumbled over the word her lady had used. ''. . . 'er lee-a-zon, 'at's it, ta git 'round, fer she says it's ta be a *secret.*"

Mrs. Rachett stopped beating the linen. She peered at Tilly, stared at her hard, then looked back at her laundry. "Hmmph," was all she said before she resumed beating the linen again.

Tilly wasn't fooled by Mrs. Rachett's supposed lack of interest; she knew the familiar "harrumph" meant the old woman had heard every word quite clearly and was no doubt deciding whose ear she would bend first with her bit of newfound gossip.

"O' course, I not be wantin' to tell m'lady's secrets, but I be thinkin' someun other 'an me should know . . . ," Tilly said, allowing her words to trail off.

Mrs. Rachett hefted another huge linen over the line. "Scat," she muttered to Tilly, scowling with earnest.

Tilly did just that. She ran for the house, quickly slipping inside the side door. Mrs. Rachett was a nasty old woman, to be sure, but she was also a gossip of the highest order. Tilly had no doubt but by sundown word would be spread through Derbyshire about Lady Lissa's liaison with the Heartless Lord Wylde.

Feeling as though she'd done a great deed for the day, Tilly popped into the kitchens, intending to pilfer a sweetcake from Cook's store. She was blasted hungry from all her running about and the excitement at the riverbank. Surely she had a few minutes to prop up her toes and quiet her rumbling stomach.

Her lady would be pleased when she learned that everyone from miles around knew of the desired liaison with Lord Thingamabob . . . and no doubt Tilly would be given a special something for her part in the spread of the rumor.

What a bonny day it was proving to be, Tilly decided, and with a much-needed rest to boot.

* * *

Lissa sat beside Lord Wylde on the riverbank and watched as he flipped, for perhaps the third time, through her sketchbook. It seemed that he could not get enough of her watercolor creations.

"You are pleased?" she dared to venture.

"Your paintings appear very precise," he said, not looking at her.

"And my sketchings and journal entries?"

"Just as precise, it would seem."

Obviously he wasn't the sort to compliment overly much. No matter. Lissa had a more important matter on her mind. "So you think you might, with the help of my journals, be able to hook that trout, my lord?"

This time he did glance up, one dark brow lifting ever so slightly. "Recreating nature in a sketchbook, my lady, is not the same as doing so at the end of a fishing line."

"How true," she murmured, casting a glance at the pathetic fly at the end of his pole.

"Faith," he muttered, rising to his feet, his irritation evident. "You seem to think you could do a world better than me when it comes to tying flies. To that, I say, prove yourself."

"I would if I could, my lord, but I haven't any of the necessary supplies, not at hand, and—"

"I do. Come. Follow me."

It was a challenge, pure and simple.

"Now?" Lissa asked. *Alone?* was what she was actually thinking.

"Surely you have not lost your bravado, Lady Lissa. A moment ago you made me believe you know all there is to know about catching trout."

"I know about insects," Lissa corrected. "Trout are another thing."

"A trout eats insects. You know about insects, thus you

know more about trout than you think you do. Come," he said again, clearly impatient. "The day grows longer as we speak. If it is a bargain we've made, then let us honor it. I'll try and hook the trout that ate your locket, but first you must share with me what you know about insects. And you'll not be sharing that knowledge here."

"Then where?"

"My river hut."

With that, Lord Wylde gathered up his belongings and headed for the fallen tree, jumped atop the rotting log, then looked back at her, his eyes giving away nothing.

Lissa debated the idea of following him to some secluded river retreat—but a bargain was a bargain, and she was desperate to catch the trout that had eaten Langford's locket. Stuffing her journals into her satchel, she hurried to follow.

Lord Wylde extended one hand to her as she reached the log. Lissa took one look at that tanned, strong hand and instantly felt her insides whirl; she remembered only too well the feel of his hands on her, his arms about her, and of how well her body had fit against his like a perfect puzzle piece.

"I—I can manage on my own, my lord," she said.

"I believe you tried that once."

Rude of him to remind her, Lissa thought.

"If you were to tumble into the water," he continued, "you would scare the trout that lives beneath this log; the very one you hope to hook. Frighten him, and he could swim upriver in search of a new home, and might never be found again."

If it was a ploy he was using, he'd found the perfect one. Lissa grudgingly took hold of his hand. Gabriel Gordon's long fingers curled around her hand as he helped guide her atop the log, and just as Lissa had feared, his touch made her insides twirl and her cheeks flush.

He said nothing, though, merely tightened his hold and expertly navigated their way over the downed wood. Lissa had to quell the urge to close her eyes as they reached the midway point. She was beginning to feel the vertigo again, but his lordship did not give her a chance to get nauseated. He pulled her along with a strong, sure grip, and before she knew it, she was standing on solid ground once again. He did not give her a chance to catch her breath or even to mentally congratulate herself for what she'd just endured.

Without so much as a pause, he released her and set a fast pace downriver, pushing brambles out of his way as he did so. Over one shoulder, he said, "You can call forth that maid of yours. You'll be wanting a chaperone."

Lissa gaped at the back of him. "You—you know about Tilly?"

"Aye. I heard her shrill voice long before I reached the river."

Lissa's eyes narrowed. "And did you hear *my* voice, my lord?"

He shook his head, just once. "No."

Lissa felt like smiling in triumph.

"But that doesn't mean I did not feel your presence," he added.

Lissa's smile faded before it began. Drat him. He liked to believe he was some all-knowing angler of the river Dove, did he? Well, she'd show *him*, she decided.

But as they passed the spot where Lissa had left her blanket and there was no sign of Tilly, she began to panic. She held back a few paces, calling a whispered "pssst!" for her abigail as she bent down to retrieve her blanket.

There came no answer or even any telltale quivering of branches Tilly might be hiding behind. Her abigail had vanished from the area, no doubt scurrying for the safety of Clivedon Manor.

"Well?"

Lissa jerked upright in surprise as Wylde, having quietly retraced his steps, peered into the thicket beside her.

"I—I believe my abigail had matters to attend at the

house, sir," she announced, trying to appear as though that fact did not signify.

"Something more pressing than serving her lady?" He took the blanket from her hands and looped the fold of it over one strong arm. "I find that difficult to believe."

As did she, but Lissa was determined not to act flustered. "You really shouldn't. A—a chaperone is not necessary, my lord. This is Derbyshire, after all. As you know, life in the country is far more relaxed than it is in Town."

"No, I did not know."

"Ah, well, it—it is," Lissa insisted.

Drat that Tilly. She would need to get the girl in line posthaste. At the moment, though, snaring the trout filled with Langford's locket outweighed all other matters, and only Wylde and the bargain they had struck could see Lissa to that end.

"Shall we continue on, my lord? As you mentioned, the day grows longer as we speak."

Lord Wylde's dark gaze narrowed. "It does indeed. This way."

Lissa fell into step behind him as they threaded their way along a slight path, heading downriver. Eventually they turned away from the water, then headed deep into the woods, far away from anyone who could help Lissa should she have need to call for aid. . . .

Tilly, sitting in the cavernous kitchens of Clivedon Manor, held Cook's tomcat on her lap and shared with him a morsel of yet another sweetcake. It was the fifth one she'd pilfered, not counting the two she'd quickly downed before propping up her toes and clicking her tongue for the cat to join her.

She licked a bit of icing off her fingers, washing it down with a long draft of goat's milk. "Ah," she murmured, smacking her lips and allowing the cat to lick the rim of the tankard she'd poured the milk into.

What a fine morning it had proved to be. She'd overheard Mrs. Rachett speaking with Cook in the pantry, and knew the old woman had been letting the secret of their lady's supposed liaison spill from her lips. From there, word had spread to other servants who passed by, and even now Tilly had no doubt that word was being carried into town upon Mrs. Rachett's lined lips as that one had thread to purchase and more linens to buy at market this day.

Tilly scratched the cat's ears, enjoying the purr she heard rumble in its throat.

"It be a good day, yes?" she said to the cat. "But now I must be joinin' m'lady. She be havin' more 'an enough time w' 'at ogre, Lord Thingamabob."

Tilly set the cat down, ignoring a *meow* for more attention. "Go on, shoo," she said, her stomach filled and her mind on her own mistress. "I gots ta git back ta the river, I do. Can't folly all day like you."

The tomcat settled down amid a sliver of sunlight slanting through a nearby window and began to clean its fur as Tilly, her stomach filled, made her way back out of the manor and headed for the river and her lady, humming as she went.

Lord Wylde's river lodge was nestled in the deep woods, octagonal in shape, and sported two circular windows that faced toward the water which lay a good distance in front of it. A profusion of long-stemmed flowers flanked the weatherworn door, and in the morning's early light the place looked mellow and quiet and very inviting.

Once inside, Lissa had to hold back a gasp. It was an angler's paradise, filled with books that lined one wall, a massive mahogany table in the center spilling over with all manner of feathers and hooks, a cozy fireplace, another wall that held various angling poles made of Jamaican and African greenheart and even British Guyana lancewood, and another wall that housed a tier of shelves littered with wooden reels of various craftsmanship and sizes, nets, baskets, and sheepskin pierced with flies not yet cast.

"You created all of this, my lord?"

"No," said Lord Wylde as he set his pole against the door jamb. He motioned Lissa deeper inside, then shut the door. "This retreat was part and parcel of the land I purchased."

"Oh . . . yes, of course," she murmured, looking about her with eager intensity, and remembering the previous owner of the spread. "Lord Markham's family owned the property prior to your arrival. The man, I once heard my father say, was a remarkable fly angler. He and my father used to fish together years ago, before I was born. He suffered an attack of the heart a year after his wife's death. He didn't do much angling, or even socializing, after that, so I had no chance to meet him. Obviously, though, he spent a great deal of time here, with his angling supplies. I did not know that his family kept his stores intact, or even that you would have done so once you purchased this estate."

"I've a great interest in angling," Wylde explained. "In fact, that interest is what prompted me to settle along the Dove River—that, and my penchant to be alone."

Lissa glanced at him. "You prefer solitude, my lord?"

His dark gaze flickered. "Something akin to that."

He nodded toward the workbench that was constructed of mahogany and was a magnificent table to say the least. Two benches ran along either side of its massive bulk, and atop it was spread a veritable treasure of angling supplies.

"Markham's, I suppose?" she ventured.

"All his. Untouched until the day I came here."

Lissa moved forward, rounding the huge table. " 'Tis quite a collection."

"Is it?"

She nodded, letting out her breath over the sight of it all. "Indeed. There are feathers here that cannot be found along the Dove. And these hooks?" She reached for a particularly shiny silver one that was small and very fine. "They have been fashioned by a master craftsman. She took a moment to appreciate the beauty of them all.

"Continue," Wylde said, rounding the table to stand beside her.

Lissa looked up, taken aback by the sheer nearness of him, and by his deep, husky tone. She had to moisten her lips before she spoke. "You are asking my opinion of all of this, my lord?"

"I am."

"It is impressive, certainly; a true angler's beloved collection."

"And?"

She knew what he was asking. "And you've everything here, sir, to become a most accomplished angler," she assured him.

"Save *your* knowledge to put it all together and make a success of it."

Lissa had to touch the tip of her tongue to her lips again. His penetrating gaze, his voice, his closeness, and especially the masculine, clean scent of him were wreaking havoc with her insides. In fact, she didn't know how long she could manage to stand so near to him and act as though nothing was amiss with her heartbeat. Truth of the matter was, her heart was pounding an uncomforting yet thrilling beat, and her blood felt as though it was roaring through her veins.

He absently ran one hand through the shagged lengths of his hair; heavens, but his hands intrigued her. Lissa remembered again how he'd held his angling pole in that strong grip of his—remembered, too, the feel of his warmth and strength as he'd led her over the downed log. Of a sudden, she wantonly imagined those hands touching other parts of her body, perhaps commanding her as perfectly as he did his angling rod. . . .

The path her thoughts were taking was most unladylike, Lissa knew, but she couldn't help herself. Nor could she

stop. She was very much affected by the Heartless Lord
Wylde. Purely physical, these feelings were, and they had
no place in her ultimate plan. How ridiculous that she,
the daughter of a man who had taught her to be ruled
and moved by the nature surrounding her and nothing
else, should respond to Wylde in such a way!

But then again, her mind reasoned, the sixth Earl of
Wylde *was* a creation of nature, just as surely as were the
insects she loved to sketch, as the air that moved around
them was, and as was the Dove River she loved so much.
That she should be moved by the man, by his essence, was
not so startling thought of in these terms, not really.

Even so, Lissa was glad when he took a step away. She
drew in a breath of air, hoping to still her roiling insides.

"I shall be honest with you, Lady Lissa of Clivedon
Manor," he was saying now as he turned away from her.
"The last time I ever studied the art of fly angling was at the
knee of my father while standing in his study in Grosvenor
Square. I was all but ten and two then, and thought if I
mastered a cast, I could catch a trout." He turned back
toward her suddenly, adding, "But having lived the past
many weeks here in Derbyshire—and having spent all of
those mornings alongside the river—I've come to realize
that casting a line isn't the whole of the matter by far."

"Indeed not, my lord," Lissa agreed, happy enough to
glance back down at the hooks and feathers. *Anything but
look at him,* she thought. "A perfect cast will intrigue a
trout, but an even more perfect fly will be what hooks the
fish."

"So I've discovered."

Lissa felt his gaze on her. She did not dare look up, did
not dare to let him see how fully his presence affected her.
She focused on the table and the assortment of things
upon it. "You've all you need here, my lord. It should not
take long before you create the perfect fly."

"Before *we* create the perfect fly, you mean."

Lissa finally looked up at his astoundingly handsome

face. Their gazes met and held, and for a single, startling second it felt as though she had known this man since the beginning of time. Lissa knew then she should have heeded her maid's warning and stayed far away from the sixth Earl of Wylde.

"I—I can teach you what is needed for a certain fly, sir, but tying that fly is another matter entirely. It takes practice . . . and—and practice takes time."

"I have time," he assured her.

"But not I. The locket—"

"Is being eaten away as we speak."

Lissa frowned. "Twenty-four hours—you are certain that is the amount of time before the inner digestive juices of a trout will begin to eat away at the locket?"

"No, not entirely certain. It could be sooner, or later. It depends."

"It depends on what, my lord?"

"A number of things. What the locket is fashioned of, for one, and on the trout, I s'pose—what it ate before and after consuming the locket."

"But you said yourself the trout most likely would not feed after having taken in the locket," Lissa said, her tone a bit desperate.

"It is doubtful since its belly would feel full, but I could be wrong."

"And are you ever, my lord?"

"Am I ever what? Wrong?"

Lissa nodded.

"Not usually," he assured her. After a moment of thought, he added, "Only once, actually—and that matter had nothing to do with a trout." With that, his mood turned alarmingly dark. He nodded once toward the work-bench. "I suggest we get started."

Though Lissa desired to question him further as to what exactly he'd been wrong about, she knew better than to do so. She immediately sat down and pulled out her journal and sketchbooks. Spreading them out on the table, she flipped through a few pages of each, finally finding the desired entries.

She peered up at him. "Shall we begin with constructing a green-drake?"

"You tell me, Lady Lissa."

By the tone of his voice Lissa could discern that he had sufficiently recovered himself from whatever bad memories his one lapse in judgement had caused him. He seemed to be ready to begin the lesson.

"A green-drake it is." Lissa reached for a square-shaped box that held a number of large hooks.

"Why that particular fly?" Wylde asked, straddling the bench, his muscled body facing Lissa's left side.

She kept her thoughts firmly affixed to what she was about. "A green-drake is taken by trout at all hours during its season," she explained. "The day can be early, late, windy or rainy. It matters not."

"Then why use any other fly?"

It was an honest question, posed by one who truly did not know a great deal about insects. Lissa finally found the perfect hook; it was large and sturdy, and extremely well made.

"Just as man cannot live by bread alone, my lord," she explained, "a fish cannot live by just one fly alone. That same fish also knows that it does not have to do so, not with all the flies that breed and die alongside the water. The green-drake is a good fly, and will taunt any number of trout to surface; but it has a short life span, and even though an angler might catch a trout with one after the fly's life period, it would not do to fish all the year with such a fly."

"I see," Wylde said quietly, and then, as Lissa pulled out the hook she'd chosen, he swung his outer leg over the bench and shimmied beside her, so that their bodies were almost touching.

Lissa drew in a deep breath, expelled it, then directed

her thoughts on what was needed to dress the hook. She spied some yellow silk that had been waxed green.

"This is what we need," she said. Noting Lord Wylde's quizzical look, Lissa explained, "It is important to dye or color silks and feathers to the perfect hue of an insect's color. Lord Markham knew what he was about; this particular silk will do well for the green-drake's body."

As Lord Wylde watched, she held the hook in one hand, then began to choose dubbing from the assortment surrounding her. She mixed together camel's hair, bright bear's hair, the soft down combed from a hog's bristles, and yellow camlet. All of this went onto the hook, piece by piece, creating a long body.

Next, Lissa picked up the yellow silk waxed with green wax, ribbing it around the artificial fly's body.

"It is most important to make the body of a fly as tight as possible," she said. "My father taught me that trout can be absolutely savage when on the feed. They will strike hard and fast and can literally split your fly asunder. It is imperative to keep the body tightly woven; otherwise it will unravel and you will lose a large fish."

"What else did your father teach you about trout?"

"Many things . . . Did you know trout eat bigger game than flies?"

He shook his head.

"Ah, but they do," Lissa said, warming to her subject, relaxing somewhat. "It was not at all uncommon for my father to find small animals in the bellies of the trout he caught. Mice, moles, baby muskrats—he found them numerous times inside trout. A trout, my lord, wants something to wrap its strong jaws around, and so you must create a fly that will entice it to do so. My father was very adept at tying flies that looked similar to small mice. He called them his 'Midnight Caller.' He would often fish not at sunrise, but during the dark of the moon."

Wylde's attention was keen. "How interesting," he murmured.

"My father was an exceptional man who respected the nature surrounding him and who made great attempts to understand the habits and needs of every living creature that dwells near the Dove."

"I see he succeeded in passing on those very traits to his daughter."

"You flatter me, sir. I only know an inkling of what my father strived to relate to me. I believe it will take an entire lifetime to glean half as much knowledge as my father possessed."

She turned back to her work, Lord Wylde watching her. "What are you doing now?" he asked as she carefully picked through the assortment of hairs and feathers.

"I shall use these long hairs of sable for a wisp of a tail. And for the wings of this particular fly I shall choose what was once the white-gray feather of a mallard. No doubt Markham dyed these feathers in the root of a barberry tree and woody viss," she explained, "with alum and rain water. The color now is a very fine yellow, perfect for a green-drake. My father used to do the same. I would help him on occasion."

"I should like to meet this father of yours," he said.

Lissa stilled. "I am afraid that would be an impossibility. He—he is dead, my lord."

"Forgive me, I did not mean—"

"My father died a little over a year ago—at the very cusp of springtime, when winter was melting away and the earth beginning to blossom. I rather like to believe it was his choice to die at such a time."

Lissa fought back the tears that threatened her. Even with the passage of a year, she had not yet learned how to stop the tears. Perhaps she never would.

She concentrated doubly hard on tying the fly, recalling every minute detail her father had taught her. When she was done, she secured the handmade fly with a strong thread and a tiny, expert knot.

"There," she said, " 'tis finished. A perfect green-drake."

"Beautiful."

Something in the tone of Wylde's voice made Lissa look up from her handiwork. She realized that he was looking not at the fly, but directly at *her*.

"My lord?" she ventured, her body tingling oddly beneath his close scrutiny.

"Perfectly perfect," he murmured, as though thinking aloud and not really intending for her to hear the words.

He reached up, transfixed, his right hand brushing lightly against a soft spit of curl that folded against Lissa's cheek. His black eyes devoured every feature of her face, the long column of her slender neck.

"Almost too perfect, in fact," he said, his voice deep and dark and sending the ripple of a chill down Lissa's spine.

She shifted nervously upon the bench. "My lord?" she said again, feeling innately that he was experiencing some sort of internal epiphany.

"Tell me," he demanded bluntly, "were you lying in wait for me alongside the river's edge, Lady Lissa of Clivedon Manor? More to the point, are you here now, in my lodge, for some purpose other than retrieving a presumably precious locket—a locket, alas, that you cannot even fully describe?"

Chapter 4

For the first time that day Lissa saw very clearly why the sixth Earl of Wylde had earned the title of Heartless. It seemed he had no care for subtlety, did not give a whit about verbally challenging anyone, and—most unsettling of all—he had a way of looking through another person, as though into their very soul.

"Are you doubting my sincerity, sir?" Lissa asked.

"I am questioning your purpose. Here. *With me.*"

"As we both know, I—I merely accompanied you to teach the rudiments of tying a handmade fly."

"And before that, at the water's edge?"

Lissa eyed him warily, wondering where the stream of his questions was winding. "I often spend the early morning hours sketching alongside the river, Lord Wylde. I have already told you that."

"Then, why have I never seen you before today?"

"Perhaps we . . . we simply managed to miss each other on our individual morning outings."

"But not *this* morning," he pointed out.

"Really, sir, your questions seem more like an inquisition. Can we not just agree that we had a chance meeting and now have made a pact to help each other?''

He eyed her closely. ''Doubtless that would please you.''

''Well, I—I see no reason to worry the issue. We simply met in the midst of pursuing our own interests.''

''Yours merely being sketching insects,'' Wylde said.

Lissa nodded quickly. ''That, and—and writing in my nature journal.''

''I see.''

She wondered if he did.

''So that is the whole of it, a purely happenstance meeting?'' Wylde asked.

Lissa nodded again. ''Yes,'' she said, having to coax the word to form on her lips. ''That is the whole of it.'' In truth, it wasn't a total lie. She'd not immediately been thinking of her desire for a pretend liaison with Wylde when she'd struck her bold bargain with him, but had been thinking instead of Lord Langford's locket and the trout that had eaten it.

''I simply wish to retrieve my property, sir,'' she continued. ''Since you own an angling rod and appear adept at casting a fly, and seeing as how I know a thing or two about the insects in this region, it seems only proper that the two of us combine our talents.''

''*Proper*?'' The word came lowly, succinctly. ''Hardly that, Lady Lissa. You've no abigail in attendance. Too, I should wonder that your household is not in an uproar at this very moment, fretting over your whereabouts.''

''I told you, sir, the absence of a chaperone does not signify—not here, in the country. As for my household, those in my employ are entirely accustomed to my penchant to go off on my own.''

He did not appear convinced. ''Even if that means being in the company of someone such as myself?''

''Such as yourself, my lord?''

''Aye, that is what I said.''

''I—I do not understand your meaning.''

"Come now. Surely you've heard rumors."

Lissa shifted uncomfortably. "Rumors?"

"Do not pretend with me, Lady Lissa of Clivedon Manor. Your abigail ran from the river because of my presence. Even *you* hesitated a moment when first meeting me."

"D-do not be absurd, sir."

"Don't you," Wylde replied.

Lissa swallowed heavily as he closed the small distance between them, his face now inches from hers.

"I have to wonder what you truly know about me," he said. "I had the distinct impression you'd formed an opinion of my character prior to our meeting at the river's edge this morning. Though you painted a perfect smile on those lovely lips of yours, I could tell by the look in your eyes you were thinking of all you thought you knew of me. Or rather, what you'd overheard about my character."

Lissa felt her cheeks score with fire. "I will admit, Lord Wylde, that I . . . I have heard some gossip affixed to your name, but—"

"I'd wager you've heard more than that," he cut in.

He was too close, his black gaze too scrutinizing. "You are overlooking one thing," Lissa pointed out, albeit rather weakly.

"Which is?"

"I do not hold much faith in stories bandied about below stairs."

He lifted one dark brow. "Oh? What of those whispered *above* stairs, Lady Lissa?"

"I give no credence to poker-talk. Besides, gossip is gossip," Lissa insisted. "I've no time for it, no matter of its origins. I do not make it a habit of repeating or even listening overly much to fantastic tales." *Not unless I want to, that is,* she thought.

Wylde's gaze narrowed. "Even if those same stories could damage your reputation?" he demanded.

Lissa had had enough. "Are you trying to intimidate

me, sir?'' she asked, stiffening, though that reaction served only to bring her face closer to his.

"Aye," he answered. "I am."

Without further warning he reached up with his right hand, capturing the back of her neck with his palm. The touch of his hand against her bare skin was startling, electrifying. Lissa had a glimpse of his black, fathomless eyes blazing with a fierce intent just before he brought her mouth to his in a thoroughly breathtaking kiss.

The pressure and feel of his mouth slanting over hers was more than she'd ever encountered in all her life. She could not move, could not think. She knew only the feel of his lips over hers, the heat of his breath on her cheek.

Rather than intimidate her, his bold kiss served to ignite a fire storm of excitement in Lissa. As if her body had a will of its own, her lashes drifted shut, and she leaned into the kiss, melting against his sturdy frame.

Wylde splayed his fingers open against the back of her neck, then slowly slid his hand forward, tracing the outline of her jaw with his thumb.

Lissa felt an immediate wave of pleasure crest and flow through her. Without even thinking she lifted her hands, placing them atop his chest, her finger curling into the fine fabric of his coat. She held fast, not certain if she'd meant to slap him soundly for his boldness or to just simply touch him.

Whatever her intent, she found herself now clinging to him, as though if she let go, she'd fall into some vast void of incoherent thought.

Lissa knew she should not be reacting to his shocking behavior in such an unladylike way, but his provocative onslaught proved far too intriguing for her to ignore.

He razed his mouth alongside her cheek and beyond, burning a path to the downy hair near her left ear.

Lissa fought for breath, opening her eyes. She had a view of the many fly-angling poles nestled in their perches along the far wall. "Is—is this your idea of intimidating me?" she tried to demand, but the words passed her lips in barely a whisper. "If so, you . . . you've an odd opinion of intimidation, sir."

His lips brushed against her earlobe. "Perhaps I have only just begun."

She should have been frightened by those words, but was not. Instead, Lissa found herself very curious as to what his next "intimidating" tactic would be.

She got her answer when she felt the tip of his tongue brush a feathery swirl against her lobe. A purely involuntary shiver whipped down her spine.

"You smell of honeysuckle," Wylde murmured.

Lissa blinked, staring hard at the far wall, trying to mentally count the number of angling poles there, to decide what type of wood each was fashioned from, decipher each pole's length and heartiness; *anything* but acknowledge the keen and newly discovered desire surging through her. It would not do at all to be physically swayed by the man, Lissa knew. She needed to keep her wits about her and not become yet another female victim of the sixth Earl of Wylde's manly charms.

"Your skin tastes of the morning's dew," Wylde continued inexorably.

Lissa, trembling, blinked again. *Two African greenheart poles,* she mentally said to herself, stubbornly trying not to become overwhelmed by his tactics. *One of British Guyana lancewood, another made of Jamaican greenheart. . . .*

It soon became decidedly difficult to concentrate on the angling rods; Wylde's mouth moved higher, reaching the shell of her ear.

Three of the poles are at least twelve feet in length; the others doubtless fourteen feet, Lissa thought, but then she heard and felt Wylde's breath in her ear. Like a fanning flame— warm, erratic—it rushed inside of her, consuming any and all of her reservations.

Lissa forgot about the angling rods. Her eyes drifted shut again.

Wylde lowered his head, nuzzling his way down the long column of her neck, and then back up again. When he reached the underside of her chin, Lissa knew for certain she was completely lost to his lordship's masterful onslaught.

His lips soon found hers, claiming them with surprising tenderness, gently teasing each corner, and them slowly easing her mouth apart. She realized with a start that he wanted inside of her.

Hesitantly, Lissa obeyed the unspoken command. Wylde's tongue delved inside her mouth, searching out the moist recesses. Never before had she experienced such stark, stunning intimacy. But she wasn't frightened. Instead, she felt a wave of curious and glorious feeling pour over her. He tasted clean. Like the cool morning air; like the nature she loved so much. When their tongues collided, Lissa felt as though her world had bottomed out and she was spinning in some purely physical realm where nothing mattered but the touch and feel of him.

His thumbs caressed her cheeks as his tongue delved deeper inside her. It seemed that a volley of Roman candles exploded within Lissa. She felt transported up and out of her body. Felt, in fact, as though she'd died and had been lifted to a place that must surely be paradise. A soft, breathless sigh escaped her.

At the sound of her pleasure, however, Wylde suddenly stiffened. Abruptly, he ended the kiss, pulling his face back.

There came a moment of absolute silence and stillness.

Lissa forced her eyes open, seeing only the obsidian depths of Wylde's gaze. He studied her for a long breath of a moment.

"Have you no fear of me?" he finally asked, his voice husky, demanding. "I could, after all, be the darkness that would steal your light . . . could be a man of scarce morals . . . someone who could eat you alive."

Lissa felt herself blush crimson. How could she charge him with possessing no morals when she herself had allowed him to kiss her so intimately?

"You—you do not seem so terrible at the moment," she whispered honestly, "and I doubt you could be so . . . so heartless as to do the things you just said."

The moment the word "heartless" passed her lips, Lissa wished she could snatch it back.

Wylde's gaze instantly shuttered. His body stiffened. *"Faith,"* he muttered. He reached up and firmly guided Lissa's hands away from where they had been anchored against his chest. "I suggest you take yourself home. *Now.* Before either of us says or does something more we might come to regret."

He might just as well have thrown a bucket of icy river water in her face.

Lissa felt her entire body burn with a hot blush, caused not only by her careless word choice, but also because of her wanton behavior thus far. She immediately dropped her hands to her lap and clasped them tight together. She felt Wylder's hard gaze on her.

"You must think the worst of me, sir," she whispered, feeling miserable inside, "but I—I should like you to know that wh-what I just allowed to transpire between the two of us is . . . is something I've never done in my life before today."

"No?" he asked.

"No," she said, feeling the shame burn deep, deep inside of her—though not nearly as deep as the effect of his kisses had gone.

Wylde touched one finger to her chin, forcing her to look up to him.

Lissa thoroughly expected another tongue lashing. It never came.

"For what it is worth, I never for one second thought otherwise," he said.

Lissa didn't know whether to feel relieved or even more miserable. Was his comment meant to soothe—or did it indicate that her return kisses had been lacking, even schoolgirlish?

She had no idea, and at the moment, since she'd so willingly allowed her good sense to fly with the wind, she did not dare to dissect the issue further. Too, she needed Lord Wylde to help her catch the trout that had eaten Lord Langford's locket and also needed his presence to help ward off her many suitors. It was best that she just get beyond this uncomfortable moment and never, ever, let herself lose control with him again.

"Yes, well," Lissa said, clearing her throat and pulling back from the touch of his finger against her chin, "I—I think it wise we both forget about that—that bit of business. We should just agree that I, er, rather, the *both* of us, suffered a momentary lapse of good judgement, sir."

Wylde seemed not so eager to sweep their kisses under the rug. He lifted one brow. "So that is what it was?" he asked far too slowly, the sound of his voice doing odd things to the rhythm of Lissa's heartbeat. " 'A bit of business . . . a lapse of good judgement'?"

"Entirely," she insisted, even though her body claimed otherwise. "I suggest we endeavor to continue on with our original pact. In fact, we should do so immediately."

Before Wylde could gainsay her—or worse, announce that their pact was null and void due to her shocking lapse of ladylike behavior and his own daring—Lissa turned back to the table and quickly gathered up her sketchbooks and journal, then chose an assortment of fly-tying accoutrements to take with them to the water's edge.

That done, she quickly got to her feet, managed to maneuver her way around the bench, them made a hasty path for the door. She did not wait for Wylde to open the portal for her, but instead opened it herself and then hurried outside, into the morning's light.

Once there, Lissa paused alongside the profusion of wildflowers and took in several gulps of cool air.

She was amazed that she'd raced out of the river hut like a ninny, more so that she'd allowed him to take such liberties with her, and still more so that she'd responded to his kisses with such wanton passion. What must he think of her?

She heard Wylde inside, gathering up his angling equipment. He seemed in no particular hurry to join her.

It was just as well. Lissa needed these scant few seconds alone to gather up not only her dignity, but her resolve as well.

While she waited for him, Lissa repositioned the fly-tying necessities and her sketchbooks in one hand, then laid her journal atop the pile and hastily scribbled a list of to-dos on the back page.

Directly beneath what she'd written earlier that morning, she drew a rather unsteady line, then listed the following: *Keep to course. No more lapses of judgement. None.* She added an exclamation point to the latter entry.

Wylde came out the door. Lissa flipped the journal shut just as he let the latch fall into place.

"You are ready?" he asked. It seemed that his protracted stay inside had been time enough to lessen the dark look of intent in his gaze and to also give some space to their combined lack of propriety.

Lissa felt a small sense of relief. "Very ready, sir," she answered.

"This way, then," was all he said, and he led the way back to the river, acting as though he'd not kissed Lissa so thoroughly as to make her see fireworks, starlight and sunshine all wrapped into one. . . .

As Lissa left the river hut with Lord Wylde, there was a stirring of intrigue and gossip brewing within all the hamlets of Derbyshire—one of Lissa's employees at the eye of it all. The raw-boned Mrs. Rachett, enjoying her moment in the sun, told one and all what she'd overheard about her lady and the Heartless Lord Wylde.

The old woman shared her second-hand knowledge with not only the milliner, the baker and even her godson who oversaw the stables, but also with the third cousin who could cook a duck to perfection at the busiest inn of Derbyshire, as well as her good friend who polished the pews for the rector at Ashbourne Church, with her great-nephew who often helped transport the Mails aboard the Royal Mail Coach, with her childhood friend's daughter who now baked confections at the far end of the smallest shire, and even with the newsboy from whom she sometimes purchased the print from London that happened a week or so ago in the Metropolis.

Before Mrs. Rachett left for Clivedon Manor just a scant three hours after arriving in the village, nearly everyone in every establishment and beyond had heard of Lady Lissa's scandalous liaison with the sixth Earl of Wylde, the very same who had made a notorious name for himself as a heartless beast of London Town.

The gossip grew to a fever pitch. By mid-afternoon, the lovely Lady Lissa was said to have become enamored of his lordship . . . and mayhap even *besmirched* by him.

The tale succeeded in whipping through all the hamlets of Derbyshire, skimming the very hills . . . until it seemed even the River Dove pulsed with a curious energy.

Who would have thought the exquisite, perfectly perfect Lady Lissa—the very lady who knew so many fine offers for her hand in marriage but had gainsaid them all—would willingly entangle herself in the dastardly web of a man know as the Heartless One?

Several prayers were whispered in Ashbourne Church for Lady Lissa. Even the rector knelt and offered a heartfelt prayer, for he knew what a fire storm all this gossip would create for his lovely parishioner. He'd married Lissa's parents, had christened the girl, and had been the one to stand over the graves of her fine parents. To hear that the young lady had chosen such a dangerous path worried him no small amount. He decided it was time to pay a visit to the lovely Lady Lissa Lovington. . . .

Chapter 5

Lissa looked up at Lord Wylde, who stood beside her near the water's edge. The sun was fully up and shining on them with a bright patch of heat. Since leaving the lodge, they had fallen back into a mode of trout angling and had—thankfully—left any and all mention of their shared kisses behind.

In the interim, Lissa had managed to study the flies flitting above the Dove and instantly decided that the hand made ones she'd created in the river hut were all wrong.

"If you do not mind," she said aloud, sitting on a rock by the riverbank and pulling out all the supplies she'd brought with her, "I believe I shall tie a handmade fly of my own creation."

She bent her head, getting to work.

Lord Wylde stared down at her. "What about the green-drake, and the other fly?"

"Not quite right," Lissa murmured, her mind on her task.

"But I thought they were your chosen flies."

"I was mistaken. That happens, y'know. An angler can

plot and plan all he wants before reaching the water about what type of fly to use, but once at the water the accomplished angler will always reassess things."

"Reassess?"

"That's right. Just as the wind will shift, flies will come and go. Whatever fly you thought best might not be at all the desired choice." She studied the feathers she'd brought, and the hooks as well. "Nature can be tricky, Lord Wylde. One must always be prepared."

He digested all she said. "And are you, my lady," he asked, "prepared?"

"Of course," Lissa replied. "I've brought with us all manner of feathers and threads and hooks. An accomplished angler is accustomed to forgoing his preparations and will simply allow the sight of the nature surrounding him to choose his course of action."

"So what you are saying, then, is that in spite of all your knowledge of insects, you really haven't a clue as to what will entice a trout to move toward a hook."

Lissa frowned up at him. "What I *am* saying is that an angler must prepare to be flexible in his methods of hooking a trout. And I am that. Now, if you'll just move to the side, so that I can get the best of the sunlight, I shall construct an odd type of fly that is a sum and whole of the insects now buzzing about."

Wylde indulged her, though appeared skeptical. "I see no single, perfect fly."

"Precisely," Lissa said, energized by the fact that they were now embarking—finally—on a course to catch the elusive trout. "The fly I shall create will be a collection of the many flies flitting about. We shall 'make do,' as my father used to say." She busily tied some feathers and thread around a rather large hook. "There. This is it," she said.

Wylde looked at the hook she presented him. " 'Tis huge," he said.

Lissa nodded, pleased with her handiwork. "And colorful. If you can cast it correctly into the water, it will be the perfect bait."

"*If* I can cast it correctly?"

"You know what I mean."

"No, I do not. Pray tell, *what* exactly is your meaning?"

Lissa stood up. "Cast the line with purpose, of course. This is the point in our bargain, sir, when *your* knowledge comes to the fore," Lissa said, trying not to notice that he was staring at her overly long. "I am adept only at recreating nature on a hook, not at casting. You, sir, will be the one to place the hook in the water and entice our trout to strike."

Lissa moved to get a better view of the fallen log and the water pooling around it. She spied several trout bellying-up near the bottom. "There is a trio of them there, sir."

Wylde finally pulled his gaze away from her. "Where?"

"*There.* About a yard away from the middle of the log. They appear to be slumbering. No doubt they are watching the water above them for any signs of a tasty fly."

"I see them," said Wylde finally. "And there are four, not three."

Lissa squinted her eyes. "Ah, yes. Four. Right you are, sir. And two of them are large enough to perhaps be our trout," she enthused.

Becoming excited, Lissa moved along the bank, careful not to step on any twigs that were half-in and half-out of the water. She knew that any disturbance in the water would frighten the fish away.

She knelt down, not caring that she was muddying the hems of her bright skirt, and taking care not to get too close to the water's edge. "May I suggest a long cast, one that gives the trout a cross-river view?" she whispered.

"Suggest away," Wylde said.

Lissa crouched down even more. "Yes. A cross view is best, I think. Lay the fly down atop the water *there.*" She pointed to a spot near the other bank. "Do so very gently, and then drag the fly back toward you, making a wake in the water, much like something edible swimming above the trout would make.''

"By all means, Lady Lissa." Wylde zinged out a long cast, laying the long line down perfectly and gently atop the water. He then instantly began to hand retrieve the silk line, causing Lissa's handmade fly to move like a living insect.

"That is it," said Lissa, pleased and very caught up in the moment. "Now do remember you must watch for a strike as you are pulling your line back toward you. When you are turning the fly back toward you is most probably when a fish will strike. You do not want to pull too fast, however, or you will get a short strike."

Wylde did as she instructed. He expertly brought the line back toward him, lifting the rod tip slightly and making the handmade fly move in the water as though it were alive and flitting earnestly through the River Dove.

Halfway back, the line became taut.

Lissa jumped up.

"You have caught one!" she exclaimed, extremely pleased. She raced to stand beside Wylde. "Now whatever you do, do not allow the trout to run all over this water hole. You must pull him in efficiently and with little fuss. A big trout will try and take your line all over the area, perhaps cutting your silk on some sharp rock, tangling it beneath and around fallen branches, or even cutting the line by wrapping it around its gills."

"I can take care of matters from here," said Wylde, his features intent as he focused on bringing in the fish on his line.

The trout fought him every inch of the way, flipping and splashing in the water.

"Oh, but he is huge," Lissa said, her excitement mounting. "You may very well have caught our trout, Lord Wylde!" She beamed a smile up at him.

Wylde, however, was too busy wrangling with the heavy trout on the other end of his line. With much expertise, he managed to bring the fish to the end of the downed log. He unclasped the catching net he carried alongside his belt, intending to scoop the big trout into the belly of it.

"*No,*" Lissa gasped.

He jerked his gaze to hers. "*Now* what?"

"*No net,*" Lissa insisted.

"Faith," he muttered, "I thought every angler used a net."

"Then you've been misguided. Really, sir, a net is not a natural thing for a trout. You should beach the fish atop the gravel near the river's side. A huge trout will relax if it is rubbing against something familiar. He will prove easier to deal with that way and will not try to struggle away."

Without even thinking, Lissa reached out and folded her hands atop Wylde's, helping him to guide the trout to the gravel bed alongside the river.

The sudden contact of her bare skin atop his jarred Lissa to the quick.

There was power in his lordship; she could feel it pulse through his strong, sturdy hands. She remembered vividly the feel of those large hands cradling her face as he'd kissed her . . . could remember again the feel of them about her waist as he'd saved her from a tumble into the river. Lissa felt her face heat with a strong blush.

Though Wylde was thoroughly focused on the trout at the other end of the line, he seemed just as aware of the contact of their bare skin.

Timidly, Lissa strove to get a better grip on the pole, but to do so she had to thread her fingers with his. She was amazed to realize how perfectly her hands clasped with his over the end of the long pole.

"A—allow me to aid you," Lissa murmured, embarrassed by how easily she'd dared to touch him.

Wylde said nothing, but she felt the deep heat of his gaze.

In the next instant, however, all the nervousness of touching him vanished as the huge trout flipped up and out of the water, struggling against the hook that had caught it.

Both Lissa and Wylde held fast to the pole, and together the two of them brought the trout toward them. They beached it on the gravel, bending down side by side as they peered down at the trout's body.

The fish was beautiful. It was spotted with reddish gold and blue spots . . . and it was huge—but not nearly as huge as the dark trout that had swallowed Lissa's locket.

"It isn't the one," Lissa lamented, despair in her voice.

"No," Wylde agreed. "It isn't. It is not as long, not as dark."

Lissa wanted to cry. "I had so hoped it would be the trout we are after."

Wylde studied the fish. "It is the largest trout I have ever caught."

Lissa was unimpressed. She'd seen countless huge trout.

"But it isn't *our trout*," she insisted. She got to her feet. "Take it, if you must. I can see by the look on your face this catch pleases you."

What she was thinking about were the rumors she'd heard that the Heartless Lord Wylde enjoyed slicing open the neck of any trout he caught. She'd heard that he kept any fish—no matter how big or how small—and immediately butchered it while at the water's edge, enjoying every moment of killing and then gutting it.

Lissa turned her back to the water, not wanting to watch as his lordship proved truth to the rumors and made fast work of snuffing out the life of the trout.

She hugged her arms about her waist, taking a deep breath of air, awaiting the sounds of the trout being prepared for a frying pan.

The ugly sounds never came. Instead, Lissa heard the gentle splashing of water.

She turned about. Lord Wylde was lowering the trout into the water. With a carefulness that astonished her, he quickly and expertly removed the hook from the trout's lower jaw, taking a moment to run one hand along the smooth belly of the fish as he gently reintroduced it to the river. The trout squirmed. Cradling the creature, he lowered it deeper into the water, and then, with an almost reverent unfolding of his hands, he allowed the trout to break free and swim away.

He stayed crouched at the water's edge, watching the river long after the fish darted for cover. After a moment, as though sensing Lissa's gaze upon him, he glanced back at her.

"You look surprised," he said.

"I—I thought you would keep it."

Wylde got to his feet. He yanked a handkerchief out of his coat pocket and brusquely wiped the wetness from his hands. "No, what you *thought* is that I would kill it. Immediately. Without hesitation."

His bald words slammed into Lissa. She wanted to refute the statement, she truly did. She even opened her mouth to speak, but closed it just as quickly. What he said was the truth, and though Lissa wished to deny that truth, she couldn't—or rather, wouldn't. She was already being deceitful enough with the man in her hopes of utilizing his presence to ward off her many suitors. She would not add more to it.

"I thought as much," he growled.

Wylde's gaze moved suddenly to a spot somewhere beyond Lissa. There came an irascible set to that strong jaw of his. "We've company," he muttered, nodding to the thick foliage behind her.

Lissa turned, spying the brightness of Tilly's bonnet and red curls as the maid clumsily tried to conceal herself and approach the river without being seen.

"It appears your abigail has gathered her courage and

returned to the scene where she left her lady with the likes of whatever kind of beast she believes I am.''

Lissa wanted to throttle Tilly at that very moment. The girl was actually slinking through the thicket!

Embarrassed, Lissa returned her gaze to Wylde and noted the firm set to his mouth.

"My maid is overly dramatic, sir. Please, pay her no mind. I will call her forth and speak to her about her ridiculous behavior of this morning."

"I doubt," Lord Wylde said, his voice as ominous as thunderheads, "that the chit will willingly come out of hiding as long as I am standing near."

Lissa felt a certain panic. "You do not mean to *leave,* do you?"

"It would no doubt be best for your abigail, and mayhaps even the two of us, that I did not linger here beside you." His gaze was so dark it was unreadable, but the sound of his words were unmistakably rich with something Lissa could not quite describe—anger, yes . . . but something else as well; regret, perhaps?

"But no matter what your maid, or even you, may believe of my character," Wylde continued, "I am not one to break a vow."

Lissa felt a perfect widgeon. "I never said—" she began.

"You didn't have to," he cut in.

A silence fell between them much like the blade of a guillotine. Lissa clamped her mouth shut tight, embarrassed.

Wylde took that moment to retrieve his gear. "I shall angle at the other side of the river," he said.

So saying, he maneuvered his way atop the downed log, then made fast work of moving across the water, easily jumping down to the bank on the other side, leaving Lissa and her abigail alone.

Lissa silently watched him. Even though he now stood at the opposite side of the water, she could see clearly that whatever gains she'd made with him while bringing in the trout had obviously been shattered by Tilly's cloak-and-dagger return to the river.

Lissa turned about, her teeth grinding together. "If you know what is best for you, Tilly," she said in a harsh whisper, "you will stand upright and walk toward me with your head held high, and *you will not* act afraid. Is that clear?"

A patch of white, and then a riotous red of curls, could be seen as Tilly, all atremble, rose to her full height from the midst of the thicket.

"Coo, m'lady," whispered the abigail, her green eyes wide as she stared at her mistress, "fancy 'at!"

All patience escaped Lissa. "Fancy *what?*" she demanded.

" 'At yer still alive, o'course—beggin' yer pardon."

"You should be begging for more than that," Lissa warned. "Enough of this foolishness, Tilly. Get over here this instant."

Tilly raced to do her lady's bidding, tripping on some underbrush as she did so. She managed to upright herself, then, slowing down, very meekly came to Lissa's side.

"What ever were you thinking, traipsing through the thicket like some thief in the night?" Lissa demanded.

"I be thinkin' o' my lady bein' made so much fish feed," Tilly answered honestly.

Lissa clicked her tongue. "What utter foolishness."

"Oh?" said Tilly, peering past Lissa to Lord Wylde, who was now casting his line with a vengeance. Tilly lowered her voice even more, saying, " 'E looks the ogre all claim 'im t' be, m'lady—mean and angry and chock-full o' no good intentions!"

"Tilly."

"It be true," Tilly insisted, "just look!"

Lissa did.

Unfortunately, her maid was correct on all accounts. Lord Wylde did indeed appear to be consumed by all manner of deviltry. In fact, he appeared downright dangerous, casting his line with a growing intensity, his grip on his angling rod hard and implaccable, and his black gaze even more so.

Lissa inwardly cringed.

It seemed the beast that dwelled within Wylde was now unleashed . . . and Lissa had only herself and her maid to blame.

Chapter 6

Gabriel purposely kept to the opposite side of the river, his mood moving from bleak to black as he tossed over in his mind the maid's toe-shivering fear of him as well as his own uncouth behavior while alone with Lady Lissa in the river hut.

Whatever had possessed him to kiss the lady, and so thoroughly at that? He'd all but ravished her, and she, blast those very haunting, familiar eyes of hers, had responded with a sweet, yet wild, abandon. It had taken every ounce of Gabriel's constitution not to wish the whole thing at the devil and just claim her as his own. Gad, but she stirred within him embers of a passion best left to grow cold!

Gabriel scowled. His behavior this morning was not only inexcusable, but totally unlike him. Or rather, truth be known, his behavior had been the polar opposite of the person he'd contrived to become these past five years. Long ago he'd vowed a vow to never again be guided by the compass of his passions—and he'd kept that vow.

Until now.

In just the span of a few hours the too-lovely Lady Lissa had managed to crack the walls he had so carefully built about his emotions. She'd managed to make him feel and want and need. Unfortunately, it was the *needing* that bothered Gabriel most . . .

From his vantage point he had a clear view of Lissa's perfect form, of that bright halo of blond hair that outshined the now-climbing sun, and of her summery eyes that were far more blue than any sky he'd ever viewed. She was beauty personified.

What could she want of him, he wondered for perhaps the hundredth time since meeting her. Ladies such as herself did not go gadding about the river's edge at dawn, nor did they allow strange gentlemen to kiss them. She'd even chosen to linger in his presence instead of giving him a scathing set-down and then taking her leave, all of which would have been her due since he'd taken such liberties with her.

But she'd *stayed,* and had even cast some of the blame for their heated kisses on herself. *Now, why was that?* Gabriel wondered, his gaze narrowing as he watched her bend to tie yet another handmade fly, her books spread out near her booted feet, her maid nervously hovering about.

Certainly she'd muttered some nonsense about a trout *(our trout,* she'd artlessly referred to it, her voice beguilingly breathless every time she did so) that needed to be hooked, and one she swore had swallowed her precious locket—a locket, alas, she could not even fully describe!

Why was the locket so important?

Or could it be it *wasn't* important at all?

Damnation! Every time Gabriel tried to think through the puzzle of Lady Lissa's haunting presence, he found himself at sixes and sevens.

He strongly suspected there was something more to the lady's purpose of staying near to him. There was an edge of desperation about her. He could sense it. Gabriel, above all others, knew well of females in dire straits.

Until a few years ago he had made a habit of saving one particular and too-precious damsel over and over again. He'd promised himself to never repeat that mistake. Never again would he climb up into the boughs over a female. Not even for one so beautiful as Lady Lissa of Clivedon Manor. *Not even,* he now thought sternly to himself, *if she has the coloring and sweet disposition of the woman he'd loved too much and too fiercely in the past.* . . .

Gabriel cast his line with fierce intent. Not surprisingly, he came up short.

His scowl deepened.

By late morning Gabriel had not caught the elusive trout Lady Lissa sought, and her abigail seemed near fit to be tied. The red-haired chit had obviously heard and taken to heart all the rumors about him. Lady Lissa however, he observed, was taking great pains to act as though she had not heard those same rumors. By noon, he sensed a chink in the cool armor she sought to buckle about her.

"I fear I must return home, sir," Lady Lissa called to him. "I've a previous engagement. One I must honor."

Gabriel, now on the same side of the river but upstream, did not press her for details. The lady's life was no business of *his*. He'd come to the water to be alone. What did he care if she stayed or if she went? He decided he should be thankful she'd finally decided to take her leave.

He retrieved the fly tethered to his leader, positioned his pole over one shoulder, then traced his steps back to where he'd left Lady Lissa and her abigail.

"I hate that I must leave now, in the midst of our endeavor," she was saying, "but it cannot be helped. I have planned a—a rather small gathering in honor of a dear friend's natal day. My staff is in need of direction, and I must oversee all the preparations."

"Then go. Rest assured I shall continue to angle for your trout," Gabriel said, his own equanimity surprising him.

"You mean *our trout,* sir, don't you?"

Gad, but how prettily she said the words! Gabriel felt her smile all the way to the toes of his highly polished boots, and wondered if she was aware of her bewitching effect upon him.

"If it is possible, sir," she added, "I would very much like to renew our pact on the morrow—that is, if you do not catch the fish today. Say at sunrise? Here?"

Gabriel heard her maid's stifled gasp. He ignored it. "If need be I shall meet you," he promised the lady, though he hoped he would not have to do so. Who knew what temptation would be thrust at him should he find himself alone with her again. "If I have any success in the meantime, I shall send word to you immediately."

She smiled again. "Thank you, sir. You cannot possibly know how pleased I am that you have come to my aid."

With that, Lady Lissa glided off, her maid nervously following in her wake.

Wylde watched them take their leave, and feeling like a wretch for doing so, he found himself admiring the back view of the lady almost as much as he did the front view of her. Either coming or going she could make his knees turn to water and his thoughts become so much pap.

Once he was alone, Gabriel took a deep breath and then settled down atop the monstrous tree trunk that splayed out its unearthed roots atop the river's edge. He sat there for a very long time, thinking, mulling over the events of the morning. It was then he noticed Lady Lissa had left either her sketchbook or nature journal behind in her haste to head for home.

Gabriel got up off the tree trunk, swiped the book off the ground, then sat back down. He flipped through several pages. 'Twas her writing journal. There were scribblings of notes throughout, all written in a clean, clear hand, and each entry with a bold date as its heading.

Gabriel carefully turned pages, not really reading the words, but rather just admiring Lady Lissa's neat script.

One entry caught his eye. It was a late May entry, dated last year, and the written script was not nearly as legible as the others before it.

She'd written

> *Papa died this day.*
> *My heart bleeds.*
> *I fear it always will.*

The next entry wasn't until late June. Here, she'd written

> *Mist in May and heat in June*
> *Brings all things into tune.*

Three days later, she'd added

> *This day I went to sketch pony and foal, then picked moon daisies in Hopkins' field. I gathered silverweed and watercress in blossom, and later looked in on the linnets' nest. Four babies were nearly fledged within the soft, downy feathers. . . . I now believe there is life after death, for it was Papa who first showed me this nest.*

Gabriel closed the journal, loath to read any more. These were her innermost thoughts. Her life, actually. He should not have read as much as he had. He felt a thief for even thumbing past the first page.

He stared long and hard at the river, simply listening as the current tumbled under the downed log beneath him. Watched, too, as the air was starred by a number of flies he could not begin to name.

No doubt Lady Lissa could name each and every one. Doubtless she could also catalog each and every flower blooming nearby. A lover of nature, she was, and a student, too, carefully writing down her observations.

So what had been her purpose in meeting him alongside her beloved river this morn? Obviously she'd traversed these lands for far longer than he'd dwelled here, and yet he'd never met her until today. Someone so familiar with every plant and animal, every fly, bud, and nest of birds, would be careful enough to get out of the way of another passerby when she wanted to do so.

Gabriel could only surmise that Lady Lissa *hadn't* wanted to sidestep a meeting with him. Clearly, she had intended to make her presence known to him this day. But why? To what end?

Unfortunately, Gabriel hadn't a clue.

By late afternoon he'd managed only a few strikes but not a single catch. Near sundown he packed up his gear, threaded his way back to his river hut to retrieve Lissa's forgotten blanket, then headed for home, thoughts of the lady in his head. He took his pole, net and basket with him, intending to study Lady Lissa's fly-making skills during the evening hours, and to perhaps rewax his silk line and soak more of the silk gut leaders.

His butler, Jives, a small, thin-haired being who possessed impeccable manners but amazingly little emotional grace, met him at the door before Gabriel even managed to mount the front steps.

By the grim look on the man's pinched face, Gabriel knew there was some sort of trouble afoot, no doubt within the ranks of his hired staff.

Jives trusted few people and tolerated even fewer. He had served Gabriel's family for half of his life and all of Gabriel's, and with sheer tenacity had stayed at Gabriel's side through literally thick and thin.

Wylde admired the man's loyalty—had been thankful for it on too many occassions, actually—and had even grown accustomed to Jives's gloom-and-doom way of viewing the world and those who peopled it. The one thing Gabriel regretted was that Jives never smiled.

"You've something of great import to relay to me, Jives?" Gabriel asked as the butler immediately reached to relieve him of his angling rod. "The cook hasn't plucked a duck in the wrong way again, has she?"

Jives, looking dour as ever, pursed his thin lips. "Cook has prepared kippers for this evening's meal, my lord. Just as she does *every* Thursday."

"Ah, so that is what has you looking as though you are about to attend a wake. I know how you detest kippers, Jives. I shall speak with Cook about her penchant to prepare them."

"That won't be necessary, my lord," said Jives, a grim note to his voice. "It is not the evening's fare that concerns me."

Gabriel cocked one brow. "So it is something more dire?" He stepped into the coolness of the front hall, intending to deposit his net and basket onto the floor near the inlaid Italian table.

Jives, however, quickly scooped up both basket and net, balancing them in his arms along with the angling pole, then managed to close the door silently behind them.

Gabriel's arched brow rose higher. "Very well, Jives. Out with it," he said. "The last time you were this eager to please was when you delivered the very noxious news that all of the *haute monde* wanted my head on a platter."

Jives cleared his throat, Adam's apple bobbing. "'Tis rumors, my lord," he said in a low, graveyard tone. "I thought you should be informed of them. From *me*. Before you hear of them elsewhere."

Gabriel felt his gut tighten, then twist. It was as though a sharp and familiar blade had just been shoved into his innards.

"Rumors, hmm?" he tried to say lightly. "You and I both know, Jives, that I've had enough of rumors swirling about my head to last a lifetime."

"That I do, my lord."

"And yet you meet me at the door to fill me with more?"

Jives, looking as serious as a pallbearer, nodded. "I feel it is my duty."

Gabriel did not move. He suddenly felt five years younger. He felt, blast it all, as though he was once again standing within his father's home—now *his*—in Grosvenor Square, and Jives was informing him of a certain lady's death, the cause of which had been hideously and forever pinned to Gabriel.

Quietly, he said, "Tell me, Jives. Tell me everything."

The butler shifted uneasily. He took a deep breath. "It seems, sir, that your name has been affixed with a certain lady of Derbyshire, one who had been chastely and securely hidden from the gentlemen of London Town until recently. The passing of her father a year ago sparked a great deal of interest within the Metropolis. You see, sir, this lady is considered . . . er, well . . . 'quite a catch,' if you will. Rich as Croesus, she is, and very lovely."

Suddenly, Gabriel did not need to be told the identity of the woman. He suspected he had already met her this morning. "Continue, Jives. Get to the point."

"The point is, my lord, that this lady has managed to make it known to one and all in Derbyshire that she is embroiled in a—a . . . uhm . . . well, a liaison, sir. With you."

"A liaison. With *me*?" Gabriel was thunderstruck "Why would she do such a thing?"

"One can only assume, sir, that it is because of your famous—er . . . rather *in*famous past."

A storm gathered in Gabriel's gaze, making the butler squirm with further discomfort. "Just how did you come to that conclusion, Jives?"

The man gulped once again, but forced himself to continue. "It is said that this lady wishes to rid herself of her many unwanted suitors, my lord. 'Tis no secret to those in Derbyshire that she has never had any interest in marriage. In fact, word has it she would sooner form a pact with the devil than be led to the altar.

"And?" Gabriel asked, rather impatient now. "I fail to see where in this twisted tale *I* play a part."

"If I may be so bold, my lord, it seems very apparent that you could play a huge part and not even know it. This lady obviously hopes to pull you into her web and relieve herself of her unwanted admirers."

Gabriel thought of Lady Lissa's wild tale about a trout needing to be hooked and how he could aid her. He felt his blood begin to boil. "Now how the devil does she think *that* will occur?" he wondered aloud.

Jives, believing the question was one he should answer, said seriously, "She obviously hopes that by linking your name with hers she will scare away her suitors. You are, after all, known to be adept with both sword and pistol. Add that to the fact you've been known to duel to the finish for a lady's affection, and well—"

"That's enough, Jives," Gabriel cut in. "I do not need a detailed account of my past."

"Forgive me, sir. Of course you do not. But you *did* ask."

Wylde glared at the butler, not really seeing him. His thoughts were purely on Lady Lissa. So *that* was why she had sought him out, and why she had stayed even after he'd kissed her so passionately. Not because of some locket or a trout or even because she'd felt some stirring of emotion at his touch, but *simply* because she angled to cast her name with his and frighten off all the skirters from Town who had come to dance attendance upon her.

Gabriel ran one hand through the shagged lengths of his hair, not certain whom he wished to curse more—Lady Lissa for her scheming ways, or himself for falling so neatly into her feminine trap.

" 'Tis both distasteful and disgraceful, I know," offered Jives. "If you wish for my opinion, sir, I believe the lady is not only playing with fire by dragging your name into such a stew, but she is also placing Master Harry at a grave disadvantage."

"Harry," Gabriel breathed. "God's teeth, but I hadn't yet thought of what all this might mean for the boy."

"Of course you haven't, my lord. The news is still too

fresh. But mark my words, sir, it will not do to have all the dust of your past kicked up and spread 'round the shire. Your whole purpose in settling here was to see Master Harry grow up far away from the ugliness of your youth.''

Gabriel's insides flamed with a rioting inferno. He had lived with his own name being dragged through the mud, but he could not, *would not,* allow the same to happen to young Harry. He had spent years searching for the boy—a sweet, beautiful child who should have been of his own seed, but was not. He'd left his family and his life behind in his quest to find Harry, had been gone when his father went to the grave and his mother as well. He'd given up more than just his blood ties to save Harry from some horrid orphanage; he'd given up any redemption he might have otherwise claimed for himself.

And now Lady Lissa of Clivedon Manor, some pampered heiress who did not wish to be bothered by a few harmless suitors, had decided she would not only utilize Gabriel's name, but would also bring back into light the long-buried rumors about him that he was so desperate to keep hidden from his adopted son.

Gabriel stood in the cool confines of the great hall and felt, quite literally, as though his entire world—the one he'd shed both sweat and tears to build for himself and his son—was bottoming out beneath him. It was a sickening feeling.

"You are certain of these rumors?" he asked Jives.

"Very, my lord. Even now the lady is preparing for what is purported as being an impromptu assembly for a friend's natal day. Word has it, though, the function will be anything but informal. She has invited all the gentlemen from Town she hopes to dissuade in their pursuit of her own self. She intends to cast their eyes toward her friend. Doubtless she hopes to allow the rumors about her liaison with you to swell as well." Jives lowered his voice, adding, "Mayhap, my lord, she even hopes *you* might be in attendance. She has issued a *carte blanche* for all of Derbyshire to attend the function. Having you among the crowd would doubt-less aid her plot."

Gabriel recalled Lady Lissa saying something about her assemblage. She'd made a point of mentioning it, had just as quickly said it was to be an informal gathering—and then she'd smiled at him; a dazzling, brilliant smile. Could she have been issuing a subtle message for him to join the party?

Gabriel decided that was her ploy all along. Why else had she chosen *this* morning to meet him alongside the River Dove? Ah, but what a perfect plotter she was proving to be!

"Where is Harry?" Gabriel asked.

"In the nursery, my lord. With his governess and his fingerpaints. In fact, he is looking forward to dining on kippers."

Gabriel ignored the wrinkle atop Jives's nose at mention of kippers. "I shall sup with my son, Jives. And afterward—"

"Afterward, my lord?" Jives interrupted, since every eve-ning in Derbyshire had thus far ended in his lordship reading Master Harry to sleep and then threading off to the book room to read about trout and angling.

"Afterward," said Gabriel, "I shall be in attendance at the gathering staged by Lady Lissa of Clivedon Manor."

Jives sucked in an astonished breath of air, his nostrils pinching together with the act. "You *know* of the lady, my lord?"

"I know of her," Gabriel said, leaving it at that. "See that my mount is readied at precisely nine o'clock. And I'll be wearing black this evening."

"Of course, my lord," the dour Jives agreed. "Whatever is your wish. Black will be most fitting, I am certain."

Gabriel watched as his butler took his leave. He soon stood alone in the cavernous hall of his new home, holding only Lissa's journal and her blanket. Both smelled of her. Like honeysuckle, and in full bloom, to be sure.

Gabriel scowled. He did not like being played for a fool.

So, Lady Lissa sought a suitor who would scare away all others, did she? She wanted a black mark smeared across her good name, one that would be forgiven once she extricated herself from his presence, hmm? Well, Gabriel could regale her with that. In spades!

He realized how reckless he was feeling, but ignored it. The lady had tossed him a challenge, one he was in a foul mood to meet. She should know better than to try and use him to her own advantage. And if she didn't know it, God's truth, he'd teach her! He would never again be anyone's performer on a string. He'd done that once and had lived to regret it. This time, he would turn the tables.

With that thought in mind, Gabriel headed upstairs to his son.

Chapter 7

Lissa noted that her maid visibly relaxed once they were free of the coppice of trees and walking among the manicured lawns of Clivedon Manor. Tilly even began to hum a sprightly tune and looked for all the world like the proverbial cat that had drunk deep of the cream. Lissa eyed the girl suspiciously.

"What ever has put you in such a cheerful mood, Tilly? While at the river, you seemed as like to jump out of your skin."

"La, m'lady," said Tilly, " 'ow was I ta know 'is lordship wud allow you ta leave 'is side with such ease? I be afeared 'e wud try and keep m'lady wi' 'im all night long. I just be glad the 'eartless One proved naught ta be a ogre."

"You are not to refer to Lord Wylde as 'the Heartless One,' or even an ogre, do you hear?" Lissa snapped, feeling an inexplicably strong urge to come to the aid of Lord Wylde's character.

Tilly nodded her head with a bit too much vigor. "I 'ears, m'lady."

"Further, his lordship would *hardly* detain me for the

day, Tilly, or even the night for that matter. Why would you say such a thing?"

"Coo, m'lady, but you be tellin' me yerself this morn 'ow 'is lordship be a ne'er-do-well blacksheep, and 'ow you be needin' someone ta darken yer name fer a time."

Lissa came to a sudden stop, taking her abigail by one arm. She felt guilty about her ridiculous plot to use Lord Wylde's blackened past to her own advantage. Now that she'd met the man, she knew she could not carry out such a plot. More to the point, now that he'd *kissed* her with such heady passion—and she'd *responded* to those kisses— she did not dare do such a thing.

Lissa trembled inside to imagine what a man who could kiss with such intensity would do to a female who sought to make a dupe of him! She needed to scotch her plan and do so posthaste.

"About what I said this morning, Tilly," Lissa began, her mind in a turmoil, "you—you are to forget I ever uttered such words, is that clear?"

Tilly squinted up at her. "Which words be 'at, m'lady?"

"About Lord Wylde, of course," Lissa said impatiently, embarrassment gripping her.

" 'Bout 'is lordship being a dangerous sort?"

"Yes, precisely. I—I should not have spoken so freely about his past when in fact I actually know very little of what has truly transpired in his life. You will forget I ever said he could be a loose cannon, yes?"

Tilly looked relieved. "Coo, m'lady, me chaffer be mum, I vow." The maid brightened as Lissa released her, and they continued their paces homeward. The maid even began to hum again.

Lissa found the tune irritating. She was still thinking of Lord Wylde. Of his kisses. His touch.

They reached the back entrance of the manor house. A wagon laden with extra goods for the birthday celebration was just about to be unloaded. Lissa's household staff was not a large one, but it appeared that all of them had been pressed into service in the unloading and carting inside of the many parcels and goods.

"Coo, m'lady," gasped Tilly, "look at it all! May I go an' 'elp? Maybe peek inside a few packages?"

Lissa, momentarily forgetting about his lordship and the passionate discoveries she'd had while in his embrace, smiled at her maid, nodding her approval for the abigail to help the others. "I fear I was a bit overzealous in my plans for the night's festivities, Tilly. Yes, by all means do help. And then spread word that I would like to meet with the staff within the hour."

"It be a bonny party ye planned fer yer friend," Tilly said, enthusiasm in her voice. She made a step to hurry off, but paused a moment, saying quickly, "Oh, 'bout whut I am ta ferget concernin' Lord Thingamabob? Fer a minute, m'lady, I feared ye wuz meanin' yer words 'bout 'is lordship bein' yer choice ta darken yer name. Glad I am ye didn' add *at* ta yer list." With that, Tilly bounded away, humming once again.

Lissa stared after the girl. "Tilly, *wait*—" she began, but clamped her mouth shut tight. The abigail was already shoulder-to-shoulder with the other servants, eagerly standing in wait to help unload the delivery.

To call the girl back would be to have all eyes upon her, and at that moment the *last* thing Lissa wished was for all of her servants to turn their collective attention toward her.

Drat, thought Lissa. Her outlandish scheme to align Lord Wylde's blackened name with her own was *exactly* what she wanted Tilly to forget! She couldn't possibly go through with such a scheme now. Not when she'd allowed him such liberties . . . and had enjoyed every nuance of his brazen kisses.

Lissa's cheeks burned with the memory of all that had transpired in the river hut with Lord Wylde. Surely she wore the traces of his heated kisses on her mouth, not to mention her cheeks and her neck.

Her face still flaming, Lissa slowed her own paces, deciding to enter the house through the front door. As she eluded the gathering of servants, Lissa made a show of contemplating the many flowers growing in profusion in borders alongside the house. She even picked a few blooms, planning to place the stems in vases for the party.

As she did so, she could not help but feel the many eyes of her staff tracking her way into the house. With a side glance she saw Tilly nod her head and then whisper a few words to the staff nearest her. Lissa then noticed that all those within earshot glanced even more earnestly in their lady's direction.

Lissa frowned to herself. She had the sneaking suspicion some rig was in train where her abigail was concerned!

An hour later, after Lissa had met with her staff and all the domestics were in motion preparing for the night's festivities, Lissa's suspicions grew. Was she imagining things or had Cook actually appeared as though she knew some secret about Lissa's early-morning adventure? Every maid employed in the household acted in the same manner, and even the butler seemed to have swallowed a canary!

Lissa was just about to go in search of Tilly when she met Aunt Prudence coming down from the landing.

"*There* you are, my dear," said Aunt Prudence, a splendiforous blond woman attired in a day gown of maize taffeta. "I'd feared you would be unavailable until the precise moment of our assemblage. Do you know Lavinia is due within the hour?"

"No," said Lissa. "I did not."

Prudence waved one thin and perfectly aristocratic hand in the air. " 'Tis true—though rather sad, if you ask me. Such a wallflower, Vinnie is! She's decided to come early and be with us when we greet our many guests. Pity, as far as I'm concerned. The girl is missing out on making a dashing entrance, but you know how she hates to create a fuss. Heaven forbid she should make an *appropriate* entrance on her own. I dareswear she intends to hide behind our skirts this night, Lis. We must come up with an alternate plan."

"It *is* Lavinia's party, Aunt Pru. She may arrive in whatever style suits her."

"Poppycock!" exclaimed Prudence, the many gold bangles on her arms tinkling as she shooed Lissa's words. "The whole point of this gathering is to give the girl a grand push toward all the men *you,* my dear, want nothing to do with." Prudence's pale blue eyes narrowed, and her gold bangles tinkled some more as she set her hands on her still-slim waist and asked, point-blank, "Or had you conveniently forgotten that fact during your grand escapade this morning, my sweet?"

"My *what?*" Lissa's gaze narrowed even as she forced down a guilty blush. "Into what sort of hobble do you believe I have thrust myself, Aunt Pru?"

"No hobble, not from what I've heard muttered about this morn. Quite the opposite, in fact." Prudence reached out and took firm hold of Lissa's hand. "The two of us need to talk. *Now.*"

Lissa's startled gasp was muffled by the sound of Prudence's taffeta skirts swishing as the older woman turned about and then propelled Lissa up the stairs, down the long hallway, and into her bedchamber.

"Really, Aunt Pru," complained Lissa as she was quickly and unceremoniously pulled into her aunt's room, "there is no need for such a cloak-and-dagger air."

"No?" asked Prudence, obviously disagreeing as she made certain no servants were afoot or lingering in the hall.

Lissa sighed, deciding to allow her aunt her head. She moved deeper into the room, scents of exotic oils filling her nostrils. Her aunt was a true world traveler and had become accustomed to exotic things. The potpourri of fragrances was dizzying—patchouli and bergamot, musk

and champac, Roman chamomile, even Chinese neroli
could be noted in the air. Her aunt loved oils and herbs
perhaps more than she did the notion of her niece being
married.

The far corner of the room harbored a large massage
table, covered with clean, thick terry cloths, and a dainty
satin pillow. The monstrosity was complemented by a sitting stool and a small sidetable, upon the latter of which
was scattered numerous pots of fragrant oils from far-flung
countries.

Prudence's massive dressing trunks claimed the other
wall, while the bed itself (transported from Prudence's
permanent home in Mayfair) was a huge creation of polished walnut, exquisite drapes, and numerous down-filled
pillows. A rich, yellow silk counterpane reflected the morning's light coming through the high-curtained windows
beyond the bed.

Though Prudence had announced she would stay with
Lissa for a few weeks following the death of Albert (her
brother and Lissa's father) Aunt Pru had somehow managed to become a permanent fixture at Clivedon Manor
during their long period of official mourning. And then,
with the advent of so many suitors from Town hoping to
be the perfect *parti* for Lissa, and with Aunt Pru deciding
she should play Cupid in the midst of all these gentlemen
and her niece, the woman had extended her stay indefi-
nitely.

Though Lissa adored her father's sister, she did not at
all appreciate her aunt's single-mindedness in seeing her
wed posthaste. But Aunt Prudence had been thrilled by
the arrival of so many suitors, and had even gone so far
as to create a list from which Lissa was to choose the most
suitable admirer.

None of the names on Aunt Pru's list had moved Lissa,
however, and now the two women seemed always to be at
loggerheads.

The sound of the bedchamber door being closed and

then locked caused Lissa to turn her attention toward her aunt. She felt like a fly caught in a spider's web; she being the fly and her aunt being the black spider come to wrap her tight!

But no, Lissa thought in the next instant. Surely her aunt would not be so set on making her a target. Her aunt was too kind-hearted for that, wasn't she?

Prudence was indeed a timeless being, thought Lissa as she watched her aunt move toward her. With her slim, but curvy form she looked no more than thirty-ish ... and yet her eyes held the wisdom of a much older woman. She was stately and gorgeous, and she favored, in her own odd way, unconventional trappings, but surprisingly never appeared outmoded.

"Out with it, my sweet," Aunt Prudence announced, apropos of nothing.

"Excuse me?" said Lissa.

Prudence was obviously in no mind for a cat-and-mouse game of conversation. "Let us get right down to the matter at hand, shall we?" she announced. "There is definitely something afoot, yet you seem bent on appearing as though you have no clue as to what that something could be. We'll start at the beginning, shall we? We'll start with you and what you have been about since—when was it you left your bed, Lis? At dawn? Ah, no, it was *before* then, if the servants can be trusted."

Lissa felt herself pale, but rallied back enough to say, "I often head out in the wee hours of the morning, Aunt Pru. You know that."

"True enough," agreed her aunt. "But why is it *today* seems to be so odd? You stayed away an inordinate amount of time, Lis."

"I merely ventured out to sketch alongside the river and—" Lissa paused, noting her aunt's skeptical glance. "I *did* go out to sketch," she insisted.

"I've no doubt that was your initial intent. But *then* what, Lis?"

Lissa could not deliver an out-and-outer to her aunt. Though the woman was too set upon pushing her to the altar, she *did* mean well.

"And then I met *him,*" Lissa finally admitted, voice turning treacherously soft as she sank down onto the edge of Aunt Prudence's massive bed, her spunk escaping her.

"Ah, now there is the rub, I s'pose," murmured Prudence. "Dare I inquire as to the identity of this 'him'?"

Lissa glanced away, out the windows, to the spreading lawns one story down, and to the dark line of woods hedging the area beyond.

"His name is Gabriel," she said, imagining him alongside the river, angling still. "Gabriel Gordon, the sixth Earl of Wylde." She glanced back at her aunt. "But you already know that. I can see that you do."

"Aye, my sweet. I have heard a murmur or two."

Lissa took a deep breath. "What did Tilly tell you, Aunt Pru?"

"Tilly? Nothing, dear. She didn't *have* to. Unfortunately, Lis, I heard the rumor from John Coachman . . . who'd heard it from the stable boy . . . who heard it from the newsboy . . . who heard it from—"

"Dear heavens!" Lissa cut in, cringing. "Obviously the domestics of Derbyshire have ears even the *walls* would envy!"

"Of course they do. Never doubt that, my sweet."

Lissa knitted her hands atop her lap. Guilt washed over her, making her feel sick inside. "Tell me . . . what *exactly* did you hear, Aunt Pru?"

"The truth?"

Lissa nodded, bracing herself.

"That you have developed a *tender* for Lord Wylde."

There came a long beat of silence, time in which Lissa decided such a thing as a *tender* on her part was not so terrible. After all, such a rumor did not involve *his* feelings—only hers. Perhaps she was saved from Lord Wylde's wrath.

"A *tender*?" Lissa repeated, keeping her voice emotionless. "A young woman is allowed such a thing, is she not? I see no harm in people repeating such a rumor."

"But that is not *all*," Prudence said. "I also heard that you and his lordship have embarked upon a *liaison*."

Lissa's heart plummeted directly into the pit of her stomach. "Oh," she murmured, and then, unable to help herself, added, "Dear God, help me."

"*Someone* ought to help you, if indeed this rumor is true! Is it, Lissa? Have you actually gone and entangled yourself in a liaison with the Heartless Lord Wylde?"

Lissa's head shot up. "He is *not* heartless, Aunt Pru. Oh, how I wish others would desist in referring to him in such an odious fashion!"

Prudence eyed her niece closely. "So you've come to know the man well."

"*No!* Of—of course not. I only met him this day."

"Yet you have already deduced he is not without a conscience," said Prudence, her mind as sharp as ever.

"He is *not* heartless, of that much I am certain," Lissa repeated.

"I see. What *other* conclusions have you drawn?"

Lissa felt her blood surge through her body just thinking of Lord Wylde. "That he enjoys angling for trout more than he likes the intrusion of people in his domain," she admitted softly, honestly. "That he is a man of few words and strong actions."

Prudence was silent for a moment. Quietly, she asked, "Are you fond of him?"

"I hardly *know* him."

"That doesn't answer my question, Lis. Are you? Fond of the man?"

Lissa's brow knitted anxiously. "I told you. I barely know the man, Aunt Pru."

"Yet you have deduced he is not without a conscience. Do you know, Lis, that when you speak of him, your voice goes soft?"

"It doesn't!" insisted Lissa. "How ridiculous. I—I merely met with the man this morning. We talked of trout and flies and angling. I—there is nothing more to be said of the matter, really."

"What of this rumored liaison?"

Lissa paled, looking back at the windows, not seeing anything in particular this time. " 'Tis just that," she insisted. "A rumor."

Prudence sat down beside her. She took Lissa's right hand in both of hers. "So all of this wasn't your intent, was not a desperate ploy on your part, my sweet? It wasn't your way of thumbing your nose at your too-persistent aunt who has been ruthlessly plaguing you to make a match?"

Lissa felt her eyes flood with tears at her aunt's perception. A lump formed in her throat. She could hardly speak, let alone think.

"Oh, Aunt Pru," she finally whispered, heartsick. "It *was*. It—it was exactly that, I am afraid."

Lissa began to cry then.

Prudence wrapped her arms about her, drawing her close. "Ah, Lis, I have been too stern in my wish to see you wed. I realize that now. I simply hoped for you to make a marriage while you are young and passionate, and not to wait too long as I have done. I would hate for you to become a spinster like myself. I want the world for you, my sweet."

Lissa hiccoughed, emotion gripping her. "I know you do. And I love you for it." She pressed her face into her aunt's shoulder. "But I have been feeling so beset lately, what with all the gentlemen from Town dancing their attendance upon me. Oh, Aunt Pru, I *did* have a scheme where Lord Wylde was concerned. I—I thought that if I created the illusion of a liaison betwixt myself and his lordship that I—I would scare away my many suitors with just one sweep. But I—I had not thought about what would happen if it actually came to pass."

"I am afraid it *has* come to pass, dear."

Lissa felt truly miserable then. "Drat that Tilly for repeating my haphazard plot! Only *think* of what Lord Wylde will do when he learns I have cast my name with his—and for such a scheming reason!" Lissa shuddered at the thought.

Prudence pulled her closer. "Perhaps it will not come to that. Perhaps nothing will come of this."

Lissa wasn't so certain. "He is not a man to be crossed, Aunt Pru," she whispered. "I felt that immediately. In fact, I fear he will not suffer being made a fool."

"But you've done nothing, really, to cast him in such a light. As of now it is merely gossip borne from a servant's lips. The world is full of such nonsense. Who knows? Perhaps this talk has gone no farther than the domestic circuit."

Lissa pulled back, tipping her tear-streaked face up to her aunt's. "You truly think so?"

"It *is* possible," offered Prudence. "After all, not all of the gentry in Derbyshire are as familiar with their servants as you and your father—and even *I*, myself, since coming here—have been with your servants. Believe it or not, Lis, others of Polite Society do not indulge their servants as your father taught you to do."

Lissa smiled a bit at this. "Father *was* a bit of a democrat, yes? I grew up to believe our servants were part of our family. And though Tilly tries my patience at times, I *do* adore her."

"Yes, well," said Prudence, "getting back to the matter at hand, no matter how far this tale has spread, given time, it may very well all blow away like a dark cloud taken out to sea by the wind."

"I certainly hope so," said Lissa in earnest.

"What *you* must do in the meantime, my sweet, is hold up your chin and smile as though the world harbors nothing to frighten you."

"You make it all sound so simple."

"You must make it simple, dear. Your reputation is at

stake. What you need do is steer clear of Lord Wylde and act as though you did not linger overly long in his presence this day. And the two of us shall hold fast to the possibility that this vile rumor has gone no farther than the servants.'' Prudence dabbed at Lissa's eyes with a scrap of lace. "Now paint a smile on that lovely face of yours and do get ready for Vinnie's birthday celebration. If I can not have the pleasure of seeing my niece married off, at least allow me the happiness of playing matchmaker for our favorite friend.''

Lissa forced a smile. "If it is a wedding you hanker for, why not orchestrate one of your own, Aunt Pru?" she asked.

"Pshaw!" said Prudence. "I am far too old to be swept off my feet! I fear there does not exist a man who can make my blood move. Now off with you. I've ordered a massage with hot oils, and you know how I *adore* a good rubbing with oils.''

Lissa got to her feet and allowed her aunt to shoo her out of the bedchamber. She was feeling better as she threaded her way to her own chambers, and wasn't even bothered that Tilly was not present to help her dress for the night's festivities. Her gown had already been laid out, as had a hot tub of water, and in truth she rather looked forward to doing her own toilette. She would dress her hair simply—a neat chignon at her nape, with a few tendrils hanging loose, she decided.

Lissa was actually glad for the time alone, for she knew that the minute she saw Tilly her blood would boil. She and her abigail had much to discuss!

Chapter 8

Several hours later Lissa and Aunt Prudence's informal soiree in honor of their friend Lavinia's birthday proved to be a grand success. The cream of country society was in attendance, as were the many eligible gentlemen from the Metropolis who had come to entice Lissa to the altar. Lissa found herself hard-pressed to be a dazzling hostess to them but studiously reminded herself that tonight was for Lavinia.

Her friend, however, looked less than pleased. In fact, she looked positively green around the gills, as though she would either faint dead away with all the attention paid her, or would merely excuse herself to go off and be ill in some quiet, dark room.

Lavinia's brown gaze held the doe-eyed look of hunted prey, and her light brown hair had fallen loose of several pins and was now hanging limply around her small, oval face. Her lips were pressed into a tight line, and her hands were doing damage to the delicate fan she held with a death grip.

"Really, Vinnie," Lissa whispered to her friend as preparations were made for the dancing, "you must try and relax. It is your birthday, after all."

"So why do I feel as though you and your aunt have led me to the guillotine and that at any moment a blade will fall?"

"Because you are nervous and naturally shy," insisted Lissa. "And is it any wonder? Dash it all, Vinnie, but your otherwise-occupied parents have forgotten you in the midst of their unending pursuit of far-away cultures, leaving you to virtually wither here in the countryside with your odious governess—a governess whom, by the way, you've *long* outgrown."

"Miss Habersham is not so terrible."

"She is positively ancient and you know it!" Lissa exclaimed.

"Very well," Lavinia admitted. "The woman *is* a tad old, and you are quite right about my parents conveniently forgetting about me and leaving me still in the care of a governess. However, that does not mean I wish to be put on display for all the titled gentlemen who have come calling for *your* hand."

Lissa was instantly contrite. "Have Aunt Prudence and I offended you, Vinnie? That wasn't at all our intention, you know."

"Yes, yes, of course I know," Lavinia replied. "And I love you dearly, and your aunt as well. Indeed the two of you are my closest friends, my bosom-bow, in fact. But you know how I hate being the center of attention."

Lissa smiled at her friend. "I also know you dream of one day having a fine marriage and that you've found no one to your liking within Derbyshire. The single Season in Town your parents gave you three years past was not sufficient, not by far, and it should have been immediately followed by *another* Season."

"An oversight on my parents' part," Lavinia said, ever the loving daughter. "They were . . . preoccupied."

"Vinnie, they were scouting for Indians in the wilds

of America! You received no word from them for *eight months!*"

"Yes, well," added Lavinia, "as I said, they were preoccupied."

"And they've been exactly that since the moment of your birth," Lissa muttered, shaking her head. "You are far too tolerant of your parents' penchant to leave you to cool your heels in this shire with an old woman as your governess, Vinnie."

"You have not fared so badly here in the country, Lis," Lavinia said, turning the tables.

Lissa blinked in astonishment, then said, "My situation is different, Vinnie."

"How so?" Lavinia asked, her doelike eyes scrutinizing her friend.

"Because I am here by choice," Lissa replied. "My father understood my love of nature and my disinterest of going to London to find a husband. You, on the other hand, have always dreamt of making a marriage and a family. Even when we were still in the schoolroom you harbored dreams of a handsome, loving man and a house filled with the children the two of you would create."

Lavinia looked away. "I—I am older now and not so naive."

"Meaning?" Lissa demanded.

Lavinia blew out a sigh. "Very well, I shall just say it; I am not a great beauty, Lis, and we both know it. I am plain and ordinary. *I always have been.* You, though, Lis, are simply lovely, and I do believe your father knew exactly what he was about when he decided to give you your head. He knew eventually the gentlemen from Town would seek you out, no matter *where* you dwelt. He knew your beauty and sweetness would not be kept hidden in this countryside you so love to traverse."

It was Lissa's turn to be uncomfortable. "I cannot help the way I look, Vinnie. I simply inherited my mother's face and form. I had nothing to do with the matter."

"How true! And therein lies the wonder of it all, Lis. You have no compass as to how truly lovely you are, and coupled with your ease within any social situation . . . well, you are simply spectacular. It is no wonder so many men from the Metropolis have come calling for your hand. They would be fools not to do so."

Lissa clicked her tongue in exasperation. "They are here only for my inheritance, make no mistake about *that*, Vinnie. My father left me wealthy beyond belief. I could exist for several lifetimes and still not spend all that I have inherited."

" 'Tis just icing on the cake of your loveliness, Lis."

Lissa wrinkled her nose. "Hardly that, Vinnie. It is the sole reason, I fear, for all this attention being showered upon me. Make no mistake that the bulk of them have come for my purse. There are a few, however, of whom I feel are honorable—such as Mr. Chesney Wrotham—and so I'm hoping you find them favorable. As for the bulk of them, I wish them to brush and lope away with all speed."

"Heavens," Lavinia murmured, "you sound so serious."

"I *am* serious. I'd gladly give up all the purse and loveliness I possess just to be wooed for the person I am."

"Aha! So a part of you *is* thinking of marriage," said Lavinia, seizing the moment.

"A *wee* part, mind you," Lissa shot back. "Oh, Vin, you above all others realize that I have always dreamt of a man who cares not a whit about pleasing others. I desire a man who is his own person, who dares to be daring, and who does not covet wealth for wealth's sake . . . a man who appreciates nature and a good day's work, who will adore his family and take pride in providing for them and loving them."

Lavinia nodded in understanding, the fight worn out of her. "I, too, want the same, Lis." She glanced about them, at the two drawing rooms that had been made one, at the double chandeliers burning bright with fifty tapers each, and at the French doors, twenty feet tall and with the rose draperies pulled back, standing open and allowing fresh air to whisper inside. "Mayhap tonight will be the night we both get our deepest wish, Lis."

"One can only hope," Lissa whispered.

Oddly enough, Lissa thought of Lord Wylde at that moment. Images of him came crashing thoroughly into her mind. She remembered him touching her, kissing her, brushing his body against hers. He'd held her so perfectly against him, had so easily brushed her lips apart and then invaded her mouth with his tongue . . . and had left her wanting more.

Lissa immediately burned with a deep-heated blush, then forcefully pushed the memory of Wylde from her mind. She could not continue remembering every moment of their tryst. If she did, she would surely go mad!

"You really didn't have to go to such great lengths just for my benefit," Lavinia was saying. "Though my parents are combing the banks of the Nile for something or other at the moment, they will eventually remember that I exist and will send a birthday gift my way."

Lissa ceased woolgathering and sharply brought her mind back to the present. "I swear, Vinnie," she said, "if you receive one more bleached bone or bit of old pottery in the post from your parents, I shall scream!"

Lavinia laughed, her brown eyes lighting with a brightness Lissa hadn't seen in a long time. "Do not judge my parents too harshly, Lis. They're in love—with each other and with all artifacts of this world."

"I just wish," Lissa said, "they were a bit more in love with loving *you.*"

"As do I," Lavinia whispered, "but I cannot change facts." She linked her arm with Lissa's, and then, with a lighthearted air, headed toward where the dancing would soon begin.

Lissa glanced at her. "Tell me, Vinnie, you haven't heard any rumors about me this day, have you?"

"Rumors?" she murmured. "What *kind* of rumors?"

Lissa debated telling all, but knew Vinnie needed no more upset than that which she was dealing with at the moment. "Nothing in particular," Lissa said vaguely. "It is just that my abigail, being overly dramatic and far too caught up in the fact that so many gentlemen have come calling for my hand, has been making mountains out of mole hills where my future is concerned. I fear she is contriving thoughts of a union where there is none."

Lavinia shook her head. "I haven't heard a whisper of anything, Lissa. But then, there is just my aged governess and myself, along with my few servants. I am not exactly in the thick of things."

"Yes, but servants tend to repeat things."

"Not mine," said Lavinia. "They are too old and too weary of the world."

Lissa wished the same could be said about her *own* servants!

Lord Roderick Langford stepped into their path then, sketching a deep bow. Both Lissa and Lavinia paused in their paces. As Lord Langford rose he gave Lissa a very private smile.

"Lady Lovington," he murmured, and then, smoothly polite, he turned his attention to Lavinia. "Miss Manning," he said. "Happy Birthday. I'd meant to wish you well earlier, but there was such a press about you and Lady Lissa that I decided to wait until now."

Lavinia, suddenly at a loss in the presence of a gentleman, turned wan, sputtering out a reply. "Th—thank you," she breathed, then looked nervously to Lissa for help.

Lissa instantly smoothed the moment by asking Lord Langford to join them as they made their way deeper into the assembly room.

"I would be delighted," he responded, offering them each an arm.

Lissa noted that Langford's grin was handsome indeed with its show of white, even teeth and full, sensual lips.

His well-groomed, wheat-blond hair had a habit of falling romantically over his right brow, and his pale blue eyes seemed always to hold a hint of interest within.

This night he was dressed spectacularly in a charcoal coat and tight-fitting white kerseymere breeches, with an extremely expensive gold pin nestled in the folds of his intricate neckcloth. He looked the epitome of a gentleman from London Town, which he was.

So why do I not trust him? Lissa wondered.

His was the suit that concerned Lissa most. He was polite but in a too-forceful way, and though she'd scolded herself many times for thinking so, Lissa could not shake the feeling that the man was not the ever-pleasant gentleman he wished the world to believe him to be.

Had it truly been only yesterday when he'd placed that damnable locket about her neck, affixing the clasp even before she could gainsay him? Then he'd gone and said that if she did not return the locket to him before the end of the Summer Season, he would know she had accepted his suit. The locket was to be their private symbol, he'd said.

Symbol, indeed! thought Lissa, angrily. She wished she had the unlucky locket with her just now. She'd give it back to Lord Langford in a moment.

But alas, the locket was gone, sitting in the belly of some overly large trout. A trout that the ever-vigilant Lord Wylde had vowed to search for in the depths of the Dove.

By the time Lady Lissa, Lavinia and Lord Langford had entered the drawing room, the small band of musicians had finished tuning their instruments and the dancing had formally begun.

Lord Langford, ever polite and socially correct, extended his first offer to Lavinia. Before Lissa realized what was happening, the two of them were dancing toward the center of the great hall. Lavinia looked a bit nervous, but Lord Langford was such a consummate dance partner that her clumsy steps were well concealed.

Lissa hadn't long to contemplate the couple before she herself was whisked off to dance the set with Mr. Chesney Wrotham, who had an embarrassing habit of stuttering in her presence, but who was a friend of her childhood and as such held a special place in her heart. She'd addressed him by his Christian name for as long as she could remember, but he had never been able to bring himself to address her in a like fashion.

"You l-look l-lovely, Lady L-Lissa," he said.

"Thank you, Chesney," Lissa said, feeling sorry for all the L's he was forced to stumble over.

Lissa glanced about them, wondering how Lavinia was faring.

"I g-gather you are l-looking for *him* to arrive," said Chesney.

"Excuse me?" said Lissa, returning her attention to her dance partner.

"L-Lord Wylde. You are s-searching for him in the c-crowd."

Lissa tried not to overreact, but her body stiffened in spite of that resolve. "What do you mean?" *Good Lord,* she thought, *has Tilly's rumor spread so far as to be dangerous?*

Chesney, his face turning beet red, missed a step, corrected himself, then blushed a deeper shade of crimson. "W-word is, my lady, that you . . . you and L-Lord Wylde are e-enamored of each other."

Lissa's blood turned cold. Surely her servants had not taken word of her foolish plot of a liaison to all the hamlets of the countryside!

"The Earl of Wylde and I hardly know each other, Chesney," she assured the young man, hoping he'd repeat her vow a thousandfold tonight. "In fact, he is not even on the guest list for this evening. Now tell me, Chesney, were I to favor a gentleman, would I not invite him to join us on this very special natal day of my friend?"

"Well, y-yes," agreed Chesney, and then, suddenly, his attention was diverted.

Chesney's gaze fixed solidly on the door to the great hall. In fact, Lissa noted, the eyes of every other person in attendance were fastened on that doorway.

She turned her head.

There, within the high-arched door, stood none other than Gabriel Gordon, the sixth Earl of Wylde.

Chapter 9

Lissa felt her heart tremble a beat at the sight of Lord Wylde standing so arrogantly at the threshold of a soiree he'd not been invited to attend. He looked like thunder on the hoof, and even from across the room his sheer height and the breadth of his shoulders seemed to dwarf every man present.

He was dressed entirely in black, the only relief being the show of snowy linen at his throat and cuffs, and the wink of a sapphire stickpin nestled in his intricate neckcloth. His hair was brushed to a high sheen and was now angled back, leaving every nuance of his harsh-planed face in clear view.

There was no denying the storm clouds in his dark gaze . . . and no denying that his eyes were fixed solely upon *her*. The man clearly had a plot of his own this night!

For an impossibly long moment it seemed that the entire room became hushed, as though all the guests in their beautiful finery were but a painting, caught and stilled by an artist's brush.

'Twas a ridiculous notion, of course, Lissa thought, for

the music continued and the dancers still moved about the floor. But even though no one physically came to a standstill, there existed a certain rent in the atmosphere. Lord Wylde would have made a quieter entrance had he simply ridden a destrier directly into their midst!

Behind discreetly held fans was being murmured a volley of words—all beginning and ending with the fact that the sixth Earl of Wylde was staging a most shocking comeback. Years after being cast out of Society due to the untimely and ugly death of his would-be bride, it was quite apparent to all present that his lordship, who had lived the life of a recluse of late, had eyes this night for Lady Lissa Arianna Lovington! The very room seemed to palpatate with an outrageous energy.

Lissa felt panic flare inside of her. Until this very moment she had stupidly clung to the small hope that the rumor of her supposed liaison had gone no farther than a few servants. Now, however, with all in attendance being interested spectators, she realized she had erred in that assumption. Good breeding and politeness had obviously stayed the lips of her many guests. It was painfully clear that everyone had merely been biding their time before remarking upon the rumor that had indeed spread all around the shire.

Lissa's face flamed. She missed a step, shook her head, then mumbled an apology to Chesney.

"Th-think nothing of it," said Chesney, his own face registering concern as he looked beyond her. "Need I come to your r-rescue, do you think? I-I may not be of Lord Wylde's ilk, my l-lady, but I am prepared to stay by your s-side should he become unpleasant."

Heavens, but Lissa hadn't intended for any of her suitors to claim they would slay a dragon on her behalf!

"Do not be silly, Chesney," she said. "His lordship has but made an unannounced appearance. There is no reason to believe he will be anything but a gentleman this night."

"Forgive me for saying so, my l-lady, but Lord Wylde

has not earned the title of 'the H-heartless One' for no reason.''

There it was again; that odious label! "That was years ago," Lissa insisted. "The man was much younger—and doubtless more foolhardy."

"From what I've heard, his lordship was a great many things, my lady. Few of them p-pleasant."

Lissa wished an end to this conversation, to this set, and mayhap even this entire *day*.

It was Wylde who managed the deed—in ending the set, at least.

He stepped into the great hall and moved immediately to the musicians. He spoke briefly with one of them—a musician who did not even miss a beat while nodding at whatever his lordship had requested—and then he backed away. Suddenly, the polonaise ended, and the lead musician announced that a waltz would be the next dance.

Of course it would be a waltz, thought Lissa, irritated, and seeing that Lord Wylde was now headed toward her with strong purpose.

Chesney, in a quandary as to whether or not he should be so bold as to claim two dances in a row with Lissa and thus leave himself prey to a confrontation with Wylde, fidgeted. His offer of assistance and to remain by her side seemed suddenly to have vanished.

Lord Langford, however, chose that moment to step between them. He held out one glove-covered hand to Lissa.

"May I have this dance, Lady Lissa?"

Lissa glanced at Chesney. The younger gentleman, relieved by Langford's interference, bowed off, then hastened toward Lavinia, claiming her hand for the waltz, glad enough not to have to meet with the fury of one Lord Wylde.

Lissa was just about to accept Langford's offer when Wylde intervened. Like a brooding cloud whipping inland from a raging sea, Lord Wylde came beside her.

"I believe the lady has promised the first waltz to *me,*" Wylde said to Langford, voice cool and brooking no argument.

Lord Langford, unlike the young Chesney, was not so easily frightened off.

"Greetings, Wylde," Langford drawled, in no hurry to back down. "Hadn't known you were to make an appearance tonight. In fact, last I'd heard, you had disappeared totally from Polite Society . . . not that anyone bemoaned your absence, of course."

Lord Wylde barely batted an eye at the insult. "You, Langford, and all other members of *polite* company can be dully informed that I have returned," he replied, steel in his voice.

Lissa was aghast at their exchange. She saw Lord Wylde's tight-lipped frown, noted that telltale muscle jerking along his strong jawline, and knew a moment of dread.

"Gentlemen, *please,*" she whispered.

Wylde's black gaze did not leave Langford's face. "I believe the lady fears the two of us might be so base as to resort to fisticuffs in front of her guests. Is that what this moment will be reduced to, Langford?"

"Not likely," scoffed his lordship. "You and your ilk have forever been beneath me, Wylde."

"Interesting," said the Earl of Wylde. "I have long held the same opinion of *you,* Langford."

Though Wylde said the words with an unruffled air, Lissa noted the ominous gleam in his eyes. Lord Langford was treading on dangerous ground—yet he seemed foolishly bent on continuing along that hazardous path.

"I see you have not changed, Wylde," Langford replied. "You remain as contemptible as I and a great many other people recall. Do not for one minute believe members of the Polite World will welcome you back into their bosom."

"I shall take that into consideration, Langford." The musicians struck a chord with their instruments, the other dancers moving into position with their partners. Wylde, taking hold of Lissa's right elbow, motioned with just a nod for Langford to take his leave. "Now if you will excuse us, the lady and I have a waltz to dance."

Langford smiled coldly, inclining his leonine head with mocking grace. "I shall beg off only when Lady Lissa insists that I do so," he warned, then turned his gaze to Lissa. "My lady? What is your wish?"

Truth be known, Lissa wished them *both* to Jericho! At the moment, however, Lord Wylde's savage black mood outweighed all other matters. She made her choice in an instant.

" 'Tis true," she said to Langford, the white lie making her insides twist—though not as much as Wylde's black stare was doing. "Lord Wylde did indeed request the first waltz."

Langford obviously did not believe her, but he was too much of a gentleman to remark upon that fact.

"So be it, then," he murmured, bowing graciously to her, his blue eyes soft on hers. "I shall claim the next dance then, and the next waltz, yes?"

Lissa, just wishing for this uncomfortable moment to be over with, nodded. "Yes, of course, Lord Langford."

Langford's private smile at her deepened, and then, with a practiced gentleness Lissa found disturbing, he lifted her gloved hand to his lips, pressing a soft kiss to the back of it before begging off. To Wylde, he said, "You heard the lady, sir. The next dance is *mine.*" With that, he moved through the crowd of dancers, heading for the side of the room.

Wylde watched him go, his lips tightening into an even darker line. "What an insufferable fool," he muttered. "You will not be dancing with him. Not tonight or any other."

"Excuse me?"

"You heard me."

"Yes, of course I *heard* you, but I do not believe what

you just uttered. How dare you even assume to tell me with whom I can and cannot—"

"Not now," Wylde cut in. "The music has fully begun, and your guests, Lady Lissa, are staring. Let us not disappoint them, hmm?"

As though his purpose had increased a thousandfold, Wylde wrapped one arm possessively about Lissa's waist, took her other hand firmly in his and then swept her fully into the waltz.

Lissa was forced to endure the lacing of his long fingers with hers, of their bodies meeting. She hadn't realized how cold she was until she felt his warm body mold with hers, had not realized what a shockingly *intimate* dance the waltz truly was until she'd danced it with Wylde.

There seemed to be just the two of them, the outer world beginning and ending with his arm encircling her waist. Lissa's nose reached to the height of his shoulders, but she saw nothing beyond them other than a dizzying blur of light from the massed candles in the huge crystal chandeliers above.

Lord Wylde said nothing, waiting as Lissa recovered herself and caught the rhythm of the dance, eventually moving to his smooth lead.

He stared down into her eyes, then moved his head closer to hers, so that his lips hovered near her left ear. "Very well, Lady Lissa," he whispered, his breath making a stray lock of her bright hair tremble, *"now* you may say whatever it is that is on your mind."

Lissa forcefully ignored how the *rest* of her body trembled with his whispered words. "I am *thinking,"* she whispered furiously, "what a perfectly improper person you are being this night, sir!"

"Easy now," he crooned, his fingers threading more tightly between her own, "your jaw is clenching, I fear. We wouldn't want your guests to get the wrong impression about our dancing together, would we?"

Lissa felt at the end of her tether. She'd been under a

huge strain from the moment she'd espied Lord Wylde standing in the doorway with that dark look of hellbent intention on his unmatchable face, and now, unfortunately, she was beginning to wear beneath that strain. If his lordship had come to queer her game, he was doing a remarkable job!

"You treated Lord Langford most shabbily, sir," she whispered hotly, not deigning to comment on his mention of her guests and what they did or did not think of her dancing with him.

"Yes, I did, didn't I? Would've liked to have done more than that, too," Wylde vowed.

"How very barbaric your behavior is this night!" Lissa admonished.

"I shan't disagree. Cast the blame on all the years I have spent in seclusion."

"I shall cast the blame where it belongs, sir; directly at your own feet."

Wylde whirled her about in a perfect turn. "Cast whatever you like, wherever you wish," he said. " 'Twill make no difference, Lady Lissa. Langford is no more than an ugly slug in a very dirty pond. In truth, I've the urge to crush him beneath my boot toe."

Lissa drew in a sharp gasp. "Sir, I will remind you that his lordship is an invited guest here this evening!"

"*Unlike* myself," he rudely pointed out.

Lissa blanched at the intended rub. "H-had I but thought you would reply in the affirmative, sir, I would have sent an invitation posthaste."

"Oh?" Clearly, he did not believe her.

"Y-yes. Of course."

"You could have issued the invitation in person," he suggested. "This morning, for instance. While the two of us were alone in my river hut . . . 'Twould have been a most opportune time, don't you think?"

Lissa's mouth formed a frown even as a definite blush suffused her cheeks. He was playing a cat-and-mouse game with her, and obviously enjoying every moment of being the cat.

"To be quite honest, sir, m-my mind at that time was not on an invitation, or the lack of one. It was instead focused on angling, handmade flies and—and such."

"Such as *what*, Lissa?" he asked, his voice whispering into her ear.

Wylde's use of her Christian name unsettled her. "The locket," she said, not liking where this conversation was threading.

"Ah, yes. Your precious locket. The thing that is perhaps more priceless than any of Prinny's jewels, or anything in Carlton House. A locket, *Lissa,* you cannot even fully describe. I should love to one day view this all-important piece of jewelry."

"Then simply catch the trout that ate it, sir!" she snapped. "And how dare you presume to address me by my Christian name?"

"I dare a great deal—considering what the two of us shared in my hut. Do you remember *that*, Lissa? Do you remember how I touched you . . . *here?*" He pulled their clasped hands toward her face, touching one gloved finger to the soft bow of her upper lip.

Lissa pulled her face back. " 'Tis clear your boldness knows no bounds this night."

He merely smiled at her—a controlled lifting of his mouth that did not fool her. Lissa decided miserably that she ought to have stayed abed this morn instead of going out in search of *this* man. To think she had at one time sought to use him to her advantage. . . .

What a perfect fool she'd been! He was beneath contempt, was, in fact, everything vile she'd learned about him over the past few weeks.

"A penny for your thoughts, Lissa," Wylde murmured into her ear.

For everyone watching it no doubt appeared as though

he was whispering some sweet nothing to her, sharing a private thought, a sultry compliment, perhaps.

Lissa stiffened. She had had quite enough of Lord Wylde's duplicitous dance. *"You go too far, sir,"* she said through clenched teeth.

"Not nearly as far as *you* have gone."

Lissa drew back, horrified, as she stared up into his impossibly black eyes. She knew then for certain what she'd only suspected the moment he'd arrived, unannounced. Her heart fell.

"You have heard the rumor," she said, a part of her fearing his verbal answer.

"Aye, Lissa," he growled, head dipping as he whispered once more into the shell of her ear, this time more insistently, "I have heard how you so boldly cast your name with mine."

She swallowed convulsively as the sound of his ragged voice funneled inside of her, reaching deep, deep down into the very being of her existence.

She pulled back, lifting her chin, her gaze wide. The man appeared to be danger on the hoof, a black-eyed devil who had swooped into her realm, intending to lay bare all of her schemes.

"I—I can explain," she began

"Of course you can," he cut in. "And, God's truth, you *will*."

It was not just a statement, but a threat.

Wylde suddenly danced her toward the French doors opened onto the terrace.

"What are you *doing?*" Lissa demanded.

"We are going to have this out."

"On the terrace? For all to see?"

"Isn't that what you wished for? For everyone to see us together, Lissa? To draw conclusions about the two of us?"

His very insistence caused Lissa to clamp her mouth shut in abject horror. She felt the eyes of everyone upon them.

Appalled, she could not believe that his lordship intended to make such a show as to waltz her right out of the room.

But he did exactly that.

He danced her toward the opened doors, twirled her once beneath them, then moved her artfully just a step into the patterned darkness and cool night air. . . .

Amidst a slanting of light from the chandeliers, he paused, gathered Lissa's body closer to his, and then he kissed her for all to see!

It was not like their kisses at the river hut—at least, not like their final kisses there had been. No, this kiss had nothing to do with eliciting a response in Lissa, but had everything to do with *making a statement to one and all of her gathered guests!* In fact, it was over before it had begun.

As the strains of the waltz played out to a final note, Wylde, his mouth still touching hers, neatly whirled Lissa out of sight from the assemblage, into a shaft of darkness at the other end of the terrace.

Lissa yanked out of his hold. *"What a nasty trick!"* she cried.

"You think so?" he murmured, content for the moment to let her back away.

"Yes, I do! What a foul and utterly devious ploy to play upon me!"

Something snapped in his darkling gaze. "No more devious than the one *you* masterminded upon *me,* Lady Lissa. Tell me," he demanded, "had you thought of forming a liaison with me before or *after* you begged me to catch the trout that ate your locket?"

With his accusation she felt a sudden, undeniable revolt of her stomach. Lissa clapped one hand to her mouth, not certain she wouldn't be violently ill.

"Dear God," she murmured, sending up a silent prayer for help.

"Obviously, plots of deceit do not sit well with you, do they, Lissa? At least, not ones that go awry." His voice was hard, unrelenting. "Allow me to take a chance at assuming what you are feeling at this moment, my lady. I suspect there is revulsion and guilt, not to mention anger. I suspect your anger is greatest of all."

Lissa sucked in huge gulps of air, forcefully blinking back the tears that threatened to choke her. She willed herself not to crumble, not to play the caught, scheming female Wylde obviously thought her to be.

"I can explain—" she began.

"I am counting on that," he cut in.

She glanced out into the darkness, feeling as gloomy as the night was black. "You must think the worst of me," she said after a long moment of silence.

"I'd like to. In fact, I ought to."

It was the tug in Wylde's voice that caused Lissa to look back at him. "But?" she questioned.

"Ah. You would like if there was a 'but' on my part, wouldn't you, Lissa? It would resolve you of your own play in this. Would make you feel better."

Drat him, Lissa thought, for turning the tables on her, for making her feel so hideously miserable. She stubbornly turned her head, glancing at a black wall of night and nothingness.

"I—I did not mean for things to turn out as they have," she said.

"Of course not." His voice was tombstone cold. "You simply wished for your name to be linked with mine. You wanted all to believe you were in the throes of some sort of new love, but hoped to do so by not having to spend more than just a morning in my ugly presence. *Admit it, Lady Lissa of Clivedon Manor, you sought to make a perfect puppet of me.*"

"No!" she insisted, turning back toward him. "That wasn't the whole of it, n-not really. Maybe at first was, but . . . but not after I'd met you. You *must* believe me."

"Given the circumstances, it is deucedly difficult to believe anything you might have to say." The heat that poured out of him at that moment threatened to smite her. He moved suddenly toward Lissa, his body just a dark shadow in the deep night.

Lissa instinctively backed away, pressing her body against the rail. 'Twas a foolish response, for she merely aided him in pinioning her to that blasted rail.

Lissa felt the heat of his lean, whipcord body pressing in against hers. His hands were on her shoulders, his thighs brushing and then stilling against her own. She drew in an astonished breath.

Wylde ignored that breath.

There was nothing but the two of them. Nothing but this heated moment.

How very foolish that Lissa had entertained the notion of using this man to her own advantage, thinking to deter her other suitors by his presumed presence in her life. Gad, what an idiot she'd been!

He was the lone wolf she should avoid! Not Chesney, not Langford, nor even any of the other men who had come to find her in the wilds of Derbyshire.

Worse, she was an even bigger fool for not considering how Lord Wylde could color her life—how one look, one *touch* from him, could make her become clay in his very capable hands.

Lissa yanked her head to the side, trying to drag herself out from under the spell he could weave about her. But she was wrong to believe she could banish the bewitching effect he held over her senses.

With all the fury of a hurricane, it hit Lissa that Gabriel Gordon, the sixth Earl of Wylde, could stir her heart like no other.

Though he was no stranger to duels, had left a would-be bride alone at the altar and had left that female alone when she killed herself, was a man who had abandoned his parents at the times of their deaths, and had made a name for himself as being nothing but cruel and dispassionate, Lissa felt her heart being enslaved by him.

Surely she'd gone mad, she thought. This was preposterous! There was no reason or even rhyme to her feelings for this man. By all accounts she should hate him.

But hate was far from her mind.

Though Lissa knew she should tell Wylde to go away, knew she should blast a world of things at him, she didn't. God help her, but she couldn't.

"Having second thoughts?" Wylde asked, holding perfectly still against her, his words in her right ear. "Think you that you ought to have thought twice about whom you ensared in your 'liaison'?"

Lissa felt tears of both fright and anger threaten to choke her. "You have no clue about what I am thinking," she gasped. "You know *nothing* about me, nothing at all."

"Ah, but I do," he murmured. "I know a great deal about you, Lissa. I know, for instance, that your body fits to mine like a perfect puzzle piece . . . that your mouth is soft, sweet and, oh, so pliant beneath mine." He stared down at her long and hard. "I also know you let it be known to one and all that the two of us have become entangled in a liaison. That is why I am here tonight. If it is a puppet you seek in me, a puppet I shall be—but on my *own* terms."

Lissa's eyes widened. She tried to pull away, but Wylde wouldn't allow it.

"I shall make this liaison exactly what I want it to be," he continued inexorably. "I shall lay claim to your time *when*ever and *wher*ever I wish. You will be at my beck and call. Your time will be my time."

Lissa flared. "Do not be daft! How ludicrous!"

"Is it?" His black gaze seared into hers, causing tingles to chase down Lissa's spine. "You began this charade. I merely intend to accommodate you . . . to be your *gentle*-man to the final degree. You have forced my hand and have literally thrust me out of the anonymity I sought. You have given me no other choice. If I am to be embroiled in a liaison, Lissa, make no mistake that it will be *my* way."

Lissa brought her hand up, and with all the force she

could muster she slapped him hard across the face. The slap exploded loudly against his skin.

"How *dare* you?" she blasted. "I have never, in all my life, been treated so hideously!"

Wylde stiffened momentarily with her stinging blow, but did not back off. "No? Well, *I* have been treated hideously in my life," he muttered, "and I didn't like it then, and certain as Hades do not like it now." He nodded toward the doors of the ballroom. "As far as your guests are concerned, Lissa, the two of us are connected, in thought, word and deed. I had no choice in the matter, no say whatsoever. Because of you and your selfish manipulation there is no going back for me. For good or ill, my name has been thrust with yours."

"If I could take it all back, I would!" she cried.

"Ah, but you cannot." He leaned closer. "You have made your unholy alliance. Now you must live with it."

Lissa wanted to slap him again, but she didn't dare. "There are those," she warned heedlessly, "who will not accept such a thing so easily, my lord. Gentlemen who will come to my assistance and who will not hesitate to stand up for my honor!"

He had the audacity to laugh—a low, dark sound in his throat. "What a coil, then, that you have created, Lissa. Gad, but you ensnare me and my blackened name on one hand—and yet encourage your many untried suitors on the other." He clicked his tongue. "You really ought to choose a side, Lissa, lest someone actually get hurt because of all this."

"Do not dare to intimate that you would bring harm to young Chesney, or—or even Lord Langford!" she returned, incredulous.

At mention of Langford, Wylde stiffened. "How I detest that man," he muttered. "The cawker is nothing more than a presumptuous skirter, not fit for proper company. You are to steer clear of him, is that understood?"

"It absolutely is *not!*"

He cursed lowly. "Damnation, Lissa, if you know what is best, you *will* make this promise to me."

"You have no say over my life!" she shot back. "And I detest your unsavory penchant to try and sway me. How dare you presume to tell me with whom I can and *cannot* associate?"

"I'll tell you how . . . It is because you have enmeshed me inside of whatever scrape it is you believe holds you tight. You've linked your name with mine, Lissa, and that is something you should not have done. You've dredged up my past, laid it bare for all to remember, and now you're about to reap the benefits of that sorry act. Though you thought I'd be a child's puppet on your string, you were wrong. What I *will* be is a perfect nuisance in your life. Before all is said and done you *will* remember the name of Gabriel Gordon."

Lissa blanched, knowing therein was the rub. Though the man was moody, mercurial, and plain ornery, she was affected by him. His kisses had branded their way into her brain, perhaps even her heart, and she knew there was no way at all she'd ever, *ever* forget him or his name. But she would be cursed before she would allow him to know such a thing!

"Perhaps it *is* true what everyone says about you," Lissa shot back. "Perhaps you *are* 'the Heartless One'!"

"My dear Lissa," Gabriel muttered, his voice void of all emotion, "you have no idea. None at all." He nodded toward the door that led back inside. "Shall we?"

"I'd rather walk a plank into shark-infested waters."

"I believe you already have," he murmured. "I suggest you start swimming."

So saying, his lordship moved back a bit, took Lissa's right hand in his left one, and then, ignoring her deep frown, turned toward the doors leading to the assembly room.

Lissa realized she had no other choice but to go with him.

Together, the two of them headed back inside.

Chapter 10

The minute Lissa and Lord Wylde stepped back into the manor house, Lissa realized that her reputation had been massacred not by the rumors of a liaison betwixt herself and Wylde, but because of the bold kiss his lordship had stolen for all to see while holding her in a sliver of light near the terrace doors. With that single deed he'd managed to upstage her plot of seeing all her suitors' hopes dashed with one fell sweep by the illusion of a liaison. Indeed, he'd succeeded in maligning her fine reputation most assuredly!

Lissa felt the undeniable urge to turn and race back outside, but Wylde's hold on her arm was far too snug. It seemed he was not yet finished queering her game.

Another set had begun, this one a quadrille. From the corner of her eye, Lissa spied Lord Langford, cooling his heels at the far side of the room. She remembered then that she'd promised this dance to him. Wylde obviously recalled her promise as well, for he quickly propelled her in the opposite direction, before Langford could move to intercept them.

Lissa's cheeks flamed, but she inwardly scolded herself not to allow her emotions to be written on her countenance, for every eye of every guest was upon her and Wylde. She would only fan the malicious gossip should she act uncomfortable at his side.

"Faith," muttered Wylde, "it appears as though you've enticed the entire male population of the *ton* to trail you into this shire! Gad, but I'd almost forgotten what it is to live within the fish bowl of the *haute monde*. Not a moment's privacy or peace."

"It was *your* outlandish kiss at the doors that has sealed their interest in us this night, sir," she reminded him sharply.

"Ah, no, Lissa," Wylde whispered, leaning his head toward hers as he neatly guided her to the side of the dance floor, " 'twas *your* totty-headed scheme of creating the illusion of liaison with me that did the deed. One must be careful what one wishes for lest it come to pass, don't you think?"

He did not give her a chance to reply. Instead, he moved her effortlessly toward the refreshment table, procuring a glass of punch for each of them.

Lissa took hold of the glass, her hands trembling as she took a sip.

Wylde reached out, touching her hand. "You should try and relax, Lissa. It will not aid your cause to appear so jittery at the side of the man with whom you've coupled your good name. A lady in the throes of new love does not, after all, tremble like a leaf in the wind when in the presence of her beloved."

"Blast you," Lissa muttered. She had had enough. She set down her glass on the table, then glared up at Wylde. *"Really,* sir, I've had quite enough of your assuming ways for one night," she whispered hotly.

"Have you?" he asked, an insufferably chatty tone in his voice. He took a leisurely sip of punch, his black eyes watching the other guests who were all covertly eyeing him and their hostess. "I take it you have not considered how I must be feeling at this moment."

"The word 'smug' comes to mind," she said through gritted teeth.

"Alas, if only it were as simple as that. No, Lissa, your plotting and planning have left me feeling *far* from smug. Devil take it, but you obviously did not pause to ponder what a seemingly harmless rumor for you would mean to me and mine."

Lissa realized what he said was true enough. She *hadn't* thoroughly considered what effect her outlandish plot might have on him, and unfortunately, due to Tilly's loose tongue, things had gone from nothing to *something* with all too alarming speed.

"I told you, sir, I—I never meant for things to get so out of hand," she whispered, feeling a miserable ache burst to life inside of herself.

"Aye, so you told me," he said, voice turning dark. "Unfortunately, it does not right your wrong."

"Then why even bother to come here at all?" Lissa challenged. "You could have simply stayed clear of me, allowing the rumor to die out. Why show yourself this night, in such a public arena? And why, oh, why, did you feel so—so inclined to . . . to kiss me for all to see?"

"Perhaps I could do no less." He took another sip of punch, looking at her over the rim of the glass, his obsidian eyes unreadable.

"You speak riddles, sir," Lissa said, not daring to decipher what emotions lay behind his darkling gaze.

"Do I? Forgive me. The last thing I wish to do is confuse you, Lissa. Allow me to be quite frank." He leaned his head toward hers, his lips brushing alongside her ear in a far too familiar fashion. "The truth of the matter is, you remind me of someone from my past . . . yet at the same time, you are like no woman I have ever met."

Lissa drew in a deep, unsteady breath at his words and their close contact. She wanted desperately to pull away, to place a safe distance betwixt them. But she could not. She felt galvanized in place, unable to move. If his goal was to surprise and unnerve her, he had succeeded.

"You—you are standing far too close to me," she whispered. "I . . . I believe it—it would be best if you did not murmur into my ear in such an . . . an intimate manner."

She felt, rather than saw, his mouth form a smile. "Ah, Lissa, you are beginning to tremble again. Where is that daring female of this morning who implored me to 'hook our trout'?"

"She is right beside you, and she is most upset by your forward ways, sir."

"Call me Gabriel," he insisted, his familiarity knowing no bounds.

This time Lissa *did* pull back. She stared up at him, her cheeks burning. "I most certainly will *not.*"

"Ah, but you will," he vowed, as though knowing something about her—about the two of *them*—that Lissa had yet to realize. "Sooner or later, you will do just that, Lissa."

Something in his gaze nicked at her very soul. She forced herself to ignore the deep-seated sensation. "You, *sir,*" she said, emphasizing the last word, "are altogether too certain of yourself."

"Gabriel, you mean." His mouth quirked with a wry grin. "After all that we've shared this day—in my river hut, and just a moment ago on your terrace—you cannot mean to continue addressing me in such a stuffy manner as 'sir' and 'my lord.' Besides, 'twould not aid your purpose to address your lover in such a fashion."

Wylde finished the last of his punch with one gulp, returned the glass to the refreshment table, then took Lissa's left hand in his, neatly tucking it into the crook of his right arm. Before she could deter him, he whisked her toward the door leading out of the dancing hall.

He did not bother to ask for an introduction to the guest of honor or even to Aunt Prudence, nor did he speak to anyone else in attendance. Instead, he managed

to compound the effects of his brash behavior of the evening by leading Lissa straight out into the empty hallway,
leaving her guests to wonder what was afoot.

Once there, he propelled her to the front door, then
dared to touch her lightly on the cheek with one gloved
hand. "Good night, Lissa," he said.

She was stunned. "So this is how the night is to end?"
she asked, angry beyond words. "You dare sweep into my
midst, order up a waltz, *kiss* me for all to see, then spirit
yourself away without so much as a by-your-leave?"

"Do not look so astonished. After all, you would not
have chosen me had you not had an inkling as to how
thoroughly improper I can be. I merely played along with
your game. You should be quite pleased with the turn of
events this evening. I gave you exactly what you wished
for—a tempest in a teapot, a liaison to outdo any and all
before it. As I see it, you should be thanking me."

Lissa felt embarrassed, angry, and confused to boot.
"You have abused me most hideously," she whispered,
almost unable to form the words. Her lower lip trembled,
so close to tears was she.

Something in Wylde's gaze shifted then. It was almost
as if he was sorry for his actions, but she couldn't be certain.

He paused, staring at her long and deeply, as though
drinking in every nuance of her features. Lissa sensed
keenly then that a part of Wylde hadn't wanted to come
here at all . . . and that perhaps a part of him did not want
to be standing alone with her in the hallway just now
because he was afraid of what might happen between them.

Surprising her own self, Lissa whispered, "I have to wonder what it cost you to step back into the midst of your
former peers . . . to come out of your reclusive hiding. By
the look on your face, I would wager it has cost you greatly.
I am sorry for that, my lord. I never meant to invade your
life, to alter it in any huge way . . . but, clearly, I have done
just that."

"Aye," he whispered, nodding, his voice suddenly

sounding odd, uneven, "you have altered my life. God's truth."

Apropos of nothing, Wylde framed Lissa's face with his hands. He looked into her eyes for a fraction of a moment, offering her time enough in which to push him away or slap him for his forwardness. She did neither. Instead, she gazed up into those black, fathomless eyes of his she was only beginning to become accustomed to, and then held perfectly still. In the span of a heartbeat, he brought his mouth to hers, gently, reverently.

Unlike the kiss he'd stolen on the terrace, or the ones she'd responded to in his river hut, *this* kiss was altogether something different. It had nothing to do with frightening her away, was not meant to make a statement to her guests.

This kiss, Lissa intuitively felt, was a glimpse of the sweetness behind the cold facade of the Heartless One. His mouth over hers proved as soft as a spring shower, as luscious as apples in season, and as thrilling as dancing the waltz for the first time with a man who could take one's breath away.

Lissa tilted her face up, caught in the pure pleasure of Wylde's unexpected onslaught. Slowly, his lips moved over hers, tasting every dreg of nectar she possessed, illiciting from her the deepest of reactions.

Unhurried and unplanned, the kiss sealed something unspoken between the two of them. Alone in the hall, with no one to judge or to intervene, both she and his lordship seemed to give of themselves.

For Lissa, 'twas a kiss that waxed their fate, melding them together. . . . For the first time in her life she felt as though she'd crossed an invisible line into adulthood.

Wylde slowly broke the contact, lifting his face slightly.

"My lord?" Lissa whispered, her mind pleasantly hazy, her insides all aquiver.

"Sshh," he murmured, touching one finger to her lips. "Say nothing. Not just yet." His gloved finger traced the outline of her mouth. "Do you know how beautiful you are when you look at me like this?" he murmured.

"Like what, m'lord?" she breathed, transfixed.

"As though you have viewed a bit of heaven . . . and as though you are not judging me—my character—as everyone else at your assemblage has done this night."

"I—I can hardly stand in judgement of you given what I've allowed to transpire between us."

"Aye, but you could and for that very reason. But you haven't. That, Lissa, is what I find most refreshing about you."

"I take it you feel you—you have been judged too harshly in your life," she hazarded.

Wylde dropped his hands to his sides, stepping back, then let out a short, self-deprecating laugh. "One could say that."

"My father always warned me those of the *ton* could be wicked with their whisperings."

"A perceptive man, your father," he murmured.

With bald honesty, she said, "I think, had my father ever met you, he would have made pains to get to know you better, sir."

It seemed that a sharp pang rippled through Wylde. "I would like to believe that, Lissa. And please, call me Gabriel. God's truth, I do not think it would be improper. In fact, I think it would be quite fine."

Lissa's heart trembled. "As in Gabriel, the archangel, the heavenly spirit?"

He shook his dark head. "Ah, no, Lissa. As in Gabriel, the man I am—flawed and imperfect . . . and the very one who came this night to aid your plot, for good or ill."

As though all this talk of his person and his past made him uncomfortable, Wylde made the final motions to take his leave. "Return to your guests, Lissa," he said to her. "Use to your advantage whatever you can of what the two of us have set in motion this day." With that, he turned, opened the front door, and was gone just as quickly and abruptly as he'd arrived.

Lissa moved out onto the stoop, feeling the cool night air steal over her body as she watched the sixth Earl of Wylde head off into the dark night, being met immediately by one of her ever-ready stablehands. Too soon Wylde's mount was brought forth, and she saw nothing but a cloud of dust kicked up into a sliver of moonlight as she watched Gabriel's shadow mix with the depths of darkness.

Amazingly, Lissa felt like crying and smiling all at once. Felt, in fact, as though she'd never be the same again. . . .

A long while later, Lissa made her way back inside. The musicians were between sets, and her many guests were milling about, talking amongst themselves.

Lissa did not need to be told what their topic of conversation might be.

Aunt Prudence came beside her. "My dear, sweet Lissa, what *ever* are you about this night? Have you gone daft— or are you truly falling in love with the man? No, don't say it. 'Tis written all over your face. You *are* in love. Or close enough to it."

Lavinia, looking flushed, chose that moment to sidle up beside Prudence and Lissa.

"Oh, Lis, just *look* at you! You are positively glowing! Do tell what it was like to be held in his lordship's arms. I don't care a whit of what I've heard whispered about the man this night, Lis, he is positively handsome and—and, well, he appears to be just the sort of person you've dreamt about!"

"*Vinnie,*" Lissa whispered, finally coming to life. "Do keep your voice down. Do you think I wish all to hear?"

"No, no, of course you don't. And never fear, Lis, even though you and his lordship will be the latest *on dit* on the morrow, I think it is absolutely thrilling that the two of you seem not to care what the world thinks! How very wonderful that you've found a man who cares not what the Polite World thinks. He simply had eyes only for you,

Lis. What woman wouldn't want such a man to fawn over her? Heavens, but this is the best birthday gift I could ever imagine; for my bosom-bow to finally find the perfect *parti.*"

Lissa blinked the dream clouds from her head that Gabriel had created, and then stared at both her aunt and her best friend. But she really didn't have anything to say on her own behalf, and certainly could not find it within her heart to refute their statements that she'd fallen in love with the sixth Earl of Wylde.

The truth of the matter was, she didn't know *how* she felt about Gabriel.

Was this what love felt like? Did one actually feel like dancing and dying all at the same time? She had no idea.

What Lissa needed was time alone to sort out all the thoughts now spinning through her head. She needed to ponder and thoroughly absorb all that had happened this day, needed time to perhaps write in her journal of her feelings, make a list of her options, and maybe even to sketch.

Unfortunately, now wasn't the time. She had a room filled with guests to worry about.

Much to Lissa's discomfort, the musicians decided then to play another set, and Lord Langford, descending upon her like a moth to a flame, was at her side even before the second note was struck.

"I believe, Lady Lissa, that this dance is mine," he said, bowing graciously before her.

Prudence and Lavinia backed away, Lavinia's hand soon being claimed by Chesney, and Aunt Prudence deciding to oversee that the refreshments were replenished.

Lissa looked up at Lord Langford. With his wheat blond hair and fair coloring he had at one time caused her to think of a gilded angel. Now that she'd met Lord Wylde, however, that comparison had changed. Though Langford was extraordinarily handsome, he did not illicit within Lissa any of the feelings Gabriel caused to stir and then flare inside of her. Though so far polite and kind in her presence, he neither pleased nor intrigued Lissa . . . and he did not make her heart flutter as Gabriel could.

Even so, Lissa danced with him. She knew she must put a bandage on all the hurtful gossip brewing. Now that Gabriel had taken his leave, she must somehow repair the damage the two of them had wrought.

"You seem preoccupied, Lady Lissa," Langford said, as they went through their steps.

"Do I?" Lissa replied. "Forgive me. I do not mean to."

"Do not tell me your thoughts are still with Wylde," he dared to utter.

"Very well then, I shan't."

Langford inclined his leonine head, studying Lissa's countenance. "Lord Wylde is a black mark on good society. He is not to be trusted, my lady."

"Is this a warning on your part, sir?" Lissa asked, her blood beginning to boil.

Langford obviously realized he was treading thin ice with her. "No warning . . . not unless it needs to be. But I take it that you, my lady, are not so foolhardy as to allow yourself to become prey to Wylde's savage ways."

"Savage? Surely you are too strong in your choice of words, my lord."

Langford dipped his head closer to hers. "The man's would-be bride sliced her wrists shortly after he left her standing alone at the altar," he said, obviously intending to appall Lissa with the tale. "Doubtless you've heard the tales, my lady."

Lissa stiffened. "I have heard," she said woodenly, refusing to believe that anyone who could kiss her so sweetly could harbor such darkness as to intentionally do harm to another person. "But since I know nothing about the woman Lord Wylde was to have married, and given the fact I know very little about the man he is, I shall not make any assumptions about what transpired in the past, sir."

Langford frowned. "Then I must be so bold as to suggest

you take care whenever Wylde is about, Lady Lissa. He has blackened the name of more than one female. I would hate for you to suffer a similar fate."

"Do be assured, Lord Langford, that my parents did not raise a foolish daughter."

"Touché," he replied, an odd, almost plotting, smile on his lips.

The set soon ended. Lissa thankfully backed away from him, then made a motion to move off the dance floor.

Langford stopped her with just a touch. "Though Lord Wylde's presence has caused me to rue a part of this night, I have decided that the evening has not been a total loss for me."

"Oh?" Lissa said, not at all understanding his meaning.

"My locket," Langford explained. "You have yet to return it. To be wholly honest, that truth buoys my spirits and leads me to believe there is possibly hope for me still in your estimation."

Lissa's right hand fluttered toward her neck. The drafted locket! It was what had brought her such unlucky luck— and it was the very excuse she would use to meet with Gabriel tomorrow at dawn.

"Ah, yes . . . your locket. We—we must talk about that, m'lord."

"When?" Langford pressed, far too anxious.

"Soon," Lissa promised. *Sooner than you'd like, I'll wager,* she thought. "Until then, my lord?" she murmured, and before Langford could gainsay her, Lissa moved away, intending to be unavailable to him for the remainder of the evening. She had Gabriel on her mind—in fact, she could not get him *out* of her mind.

Would Gabriel hold true to his vow in helping her hook the trout that had eaten Langford's locket? Or might he consider his promise null and void due to her duplicitous plot of intending to align her name with his? Lissa had no idea. What she *hoped* was that her encounter with Lord Wylde this night had not enraged him so much that he would abandon their endeavor to catch the wily trout both of them sought.

But would he even be at the river come dawn?

Perhaps more importantly, *should she be so bold as to be there?*

It would be daring of her to make a showing alongside the Dove early tomorrow morning, given the kiss he'd stolen for all to see, coupled with the more intimate kiss they had shared while at the front door of the manor.

Perhaps his lordship was just playing some sort of dangerous game with her and her virtue, a part of him wondering how far she would dare to tread along the path of thoroughly shredding her reputation.

Then again, perhaps his final kiss of the night was proof positive that he, just as she, felt something when the two of them were together. Perhaps Gabriel was as much drawn to Lissa as she was to him. . . .

Lissa's head spun with all the possibilities. Doubtless she could spend an eternity puzzling over all that had transpired betwixt herself and the enigmatic Lord Wylde this day! For that reason alone, Lissa knew she would be at the river's edge come dawn. She needed to learn whether Gabriel was concocting some sort of emotional game between them, or if he was as caught up in the energy that flared inside of her whenever they were together.

Even if Lissa *didn't* need to catch a certain trout—and soon!—she knew she would make the trek to the Dove at dawn to meet Gabriel. For better or worse, she'd become enmeshed within the enigma that was Lord Wylde.

There would be little sleep for Lissa once Lavinia's natal day celebration came to a close, she knew. Dawn, and not midnight, seemed to have become the witching hour.

A part of Lissa decided that daylight could not come soon enough . . . while another, more cautious part of her deduced that tomorrow's dawn alongside the Dove might well prove to be disastrous!

Chapter 11

Gabriel was feeling in odd spirits when he arrived home. After checking on Harry, who was peacefully asleep, he went immediately to his library. He closed the door soundly behind him, shutting out the echo in his brain of the evening he'd just put himself through.

He was amazed that he'd even set foot in a room teeming with so many members of the *ton,* with people he'd sworn never to come near again. Lissa, and her plot of a liaison with him, had clearly set him into a stew.

But even though Gabriel had set out for Lissa's assemblage in a foul and savage mood, by the time he'd led her out into the front hall his anger had begun to dissipate. And when his mouth had melded with hers, he'd experienced both a death and rebirth. He'd felt, for the first time in six years, that life might actually hold a promise for the bruised part of his soul that not even Harry's presence could help to heal. He knew for certain there was unfinished business betwixt himself and the lovely heiress who sought no suitors, things that went far beyond trout or a locket lost.

Though the lady was known for not wishing or even seeking a marriage, Gabriel had sensed in Lissa's passionate responses to him that she—*just as he*—was caught up in the maelstrom of emotions flaring to life whenever the two of them were together.

Gabriel mulled over all of this as he sank down into his favorite chair. He'd placed Lissa's folded blanket atop the small table beside him, her nature journal as well. His angling pole and fishing basket were also atop the table since he'd been of the mind to contemplate his angling endeavors this night. But all thoughts of angling paled in comparison to the puzzle of Lissa and his feelings for her.

Was he falling in love? he wondered.

Or had he simply become too lonely over the past many years and was now reaching out for any kind of companionship, no matter how preposterous?

Gabriel glanced at Lissa's forgotten blanket. He touched the hem of it, his long fingers gliding over the sturdy material. From there, his hand moved to her nature journal.

He should have returned the journal to her by now, should have taken it to Lissa's gathering with him. But he hadn't. Mayhap he'd been too angry after talking with Jives earlier . . . or maybe he just wanted to keep for a little while longer something that she treasured.

Whatever the reason, the journal was here, beside him, and though he told himself not to do so, Gabriel picked the thing up, settled back, then began thumbing through its many pages.

He moved past the notes about her father's death, about the mention of the baby birds in a nest, and found to his keen interest several entries detailing Lissa's adventurous night visits to the River Dove.

Just as she'd mentioned to him earlier that day, her father had been an angler of the night, and clearly, following in the wake of the man's death, Lissa had sought to discover some of the wonders her father had told her about.

In her perfect script, she'd written

> *There are not very many night anglers who partake of the "Black Art," or so Papa told me. The bigger brown trout, though, become nocturnal. They find the "better feed at night," Papa explained, and so become very cautious. They are also extraordinarily Bedlam-mad at times during the night, feeding with an absolute frenzy! They could be lying out within the water during the daylight, and if an angler raises his rod tip to cast, they are gone—but at night, if the trout are on the feed, an astute angler can catch them. . . .*
>
> *I decided, late last night, to gather my courage about me and head to the Dove shortly after midnight. 'Twas the dark of the moon. I needed a lantern to light my way, so thick was the pure blackness. Once I reached my destination, I was amazed at the pulse of life beating all around the river. I'd had no inkling of the energy that surged along the Dove during the depths of night! It was truly otherworldly, a place of fascinating busyness.*

Gabriel, very much caught up in Lissa's journal entries, fought down the feeling of guilt that washed through him. He was invading her privacy by reading her thoughts, but he wanted to know more about night angling for trout— and God's truth, he wanted to know more about the lady who had caught his interest and responded to his kisses with such toe-curling passion.

He continued reading.

> *After midnight, the entire structure of a stream changes. It is a different place, a beehive of activity as the air temperature drops and the water temperature drops. Papa explained to me that when the latter happens, more oxygen comes into*

the water, and therefore the best insect hatches often occur after midnight.

On this particular night, the very air seemed to thrum with insect life. I was amazed and pleased, and recall just standing at the river's edge and feeling many large-winged flies beat against my skin. The dragonflies were most pronounced. I loved hearing the thrum of their tiny wings! I espied many bats—or at least, their shadows. They swooped and swerved, claiming the night with their crazed curves. A whippoorwill sounded far off in the distance. I heard the howl of several wolves as well. Lonely calls they were, but oddly enough the sounds comforted me. I did not feel alone in the Stygian dark. I dareswear I felt very much at home.

I settled down alongside the bank and allowed my lantern to grow dim. I wished to view this dark world as a creature of the night. Following is what I noted . . .

When all cools within the Dove, the larger trout move out in the stream and find feeding stations along huge rocks or the banks of the river. Bugs and flies settle on these rocks because they are seeking heat. And then mice come, looking for food. Oftentimes, one of these mice will tumble off the rocks, into the water. A trout will sense the mouse swimming in the water, and up he goes, capturing the mouse around the tail-end and pulling it down! I was surprised at the savageness of the trout in taking the mouse. Papa once explained how trout can be perfect carnivores. From what I have seen, he was very precise in his description. I swear I could hear the trout's jaws click as it overtook its prey!

Lissa then segued into describing a particular handmade fly her father had created during his lifetime. Dubbed the "Midnight Caller," the fly resembled a mouse, was made of deer hair dyed black that was meticulously spun round the hook and trimmed, and had a tail made of boar bristle.

Gabriel, very interested in this concept of angling during the dark of the moon, paid close attention to these entries. He went over and over the words, mentally envisioned the

Dove at night, and then got up, procured paper and pen, then sat back down and took meticulous notes.

That done, he spent the next hour waxing his silk line, soaking his cat-gut leaders, and then dried the handmade flies Lissa had created for him.

Sometime around midnight he took Lissa's journal and her blanket in his arms, gathered up his angling rod and the handmade flies, then headed to his river lodge, thoughts of creating a "Midnight Caller" of his own on his mind.

It took several hours to create such a fly. Gabriel's fingers felt clumsy as he wound the deer hair and affixed it about a long, delicate hook. He wished Lissa was beside him, schooling him in the exact ways of creating such a fly. No doubt she was still entertaining her guests—possibly even dancing until dawn with the dastardly Lord Langford. Gabriel's mood blackened at the mere thought of the latter. He wanted Lissa nowhere *near* Langford.

His only balm was in knowing that Lissa, come dawn, would hopefully spirit herself to the river and meet him there, intent on hooking "their trout" and retrieving her precious locket. He hoped his behavior of this night—and the kisses he'd stolen yet *again*—would not cause her to have a change of heart.

By two A.M., Gabriel had accomplished the completion of two flies that seemed both strong in construction and true to form.

He rubbed the back of his neck, his eyes heavy from lack of sleep. He ought to go back to the main house, he knew, ought to settle in his bed for what remained of the night.

But he wasn't ready to leave the refuge of his lodge. He could still imagine Lissa's honeysuckle scent filling the interior, and for now—possibly forever—it seemed that he could recall her best while in this cozy place where he'd first touched her.

Extinguishing the light, Gabriel settled down on the

bench and pulled Lissa's forgotten blanket up and over the long length of him.

Gabriel propped one arm behind his head, staring up at a black ceiling of nothingness as he thought of all that had transpired this day, and remembered the feel of Lissa in his arms.

She alone, it seemed, held the power to unhinge him, to blast his perfectly ordered life into so much emotional upheaval, and to leave him wondering about what she was doing and with whom she was doing it.

Was she dancing with Langford at this very moment? Was her heart beating against Langford's chest as fully as it had thrummed against his own? Was her mouth looking as sweetly kissable to that windsucker Langford as it had appeared to Gabriel earlier?

Damnation! thought Gabriel, squirming atop the hard bench, his mind and his heart in chaos. He could not tolerate the thought of Lissa with Langford. He should have stayed until the final guest begged off. He should have. . . .

Bother it all, he thought. He should have done a good many things, such as tell Lissa what was truly in his mind; that she was the most beautiful, intriguing female he'd ever met. That she had the power to overshadow even his memories of Jenny, the woman he thought he'd love forever and would never forget.

He should have told Lissa that she'd managed in a short span of time to make him feel alive again, that she'd become a bright ray of sunshine in his life, no matter of her duplicitous plot of using his blackened past to her advantage. . . .

Unfortunately, he'd said none of that. Though anger had swept him into her home, his deepest reactions to the lady had made him dare only to promise to shadow her every step, kiss her passionately at her front door, and then leave.

What a perfect fool he'd made of himself.

A fool in love, mayhap.

As Gabriel drifted off into restless sleep, he wondered if his supposed "liaison" with Lissa could go beyond what she'd first imagined, and if it could metamorphose into something each of them might truly want. Come dawn, he might have a clue—that is, if the lady kept her vow and met him alongside the Dove.

He hoped she would, almost prayed for that, in fact. But prayer had not come easily to Gabriel over the past many years. In fact, prayer had become the most difficult thing of all since the death of Harry's mother.

Maybe tomorrow, Gabriel thought, he'd be able to make amends with Lissa, and to perhaps even pray again. Mayhap tomorrow would truly be a new beginning for him—with Lissa beside him.

Only time would tell.

With that thought, he finally fell into a dream-filled sleep. Pity that his dreams involved both Lissa and Langford, and with his own self drowning in restless waters kicked up by the evilness that was Langford. . . .

Lissa came awake well before dawn. She got dressed and was pacing her rooms long before Tilly's knock sounded upon her door. The abigail brought with her a breakfast tray as well as an apology of sorts.

"La, m'lady," said Tilly quietly, looking as tired and wan as Lissa felt, "I did no' mean fer my words ta bring so much trouble. 'Ow wuz I ta know 'is lordship wud hears the rumor of servants?"

Lissa was in no mood to dissect how or when Gabriel had learned of her outrageous scheme, nor was she in any mind to hash out the matter with Tilly. As Aunt Prudence had so pointedly suggested, it was high time Lissa brought her maid to heel and ceased treating the gossipy girl as someone in whom she should confide.

"Must ye go ta the river this morn, m'lady?" Tilly asked.

"Can not Lor' Thingamabob do wi'out yer presence, and ye wi' 'is?''

Lissa yanked on a pair of soft kid gloves, a warning in her gaze. "I am going, Tilly, with or without you."

"Even 'afore yer breakfast, m' lady?''

"I am not hungry," Lissa said. "Now, if you are joining me, leave the tray and gather up my satchel and a blanket. And I am warning you, Tilly, you are *not* to repeat any of what you see or hear this day, is that clear?''

Tilly bowed her head, suddenly studying the toes of her shoes. "Very clear, m'lady."

"Good," said Lissa. "God knows I have had enough of your 'help' to last a lifetime." With that, Lissa headed out of her chamber, then down the hall, intending to exit the house as quickly and as quietly as possible.

Doing so proved a breeze given the late hours of the gathering the night before. Aunt Prudence was no doubt still abed, as were the bulk of the servants. Lissa decided she and her abigail were the only ones of the manor foolish enough to be up and out the door before dawn.

Once outside, Lissa drew her cloak more closely about her. The air was cool and still wet. She felt her body begin to shiver as she and her maid took the path that led to the river.

Gabriel was nowhere to be seen.

"'E ain't 'ere," whined Tilly, finally finding nerve enough to lapse into her usual lack of decorum. "May'ap 'e be too angry ta fish t'day, m'lady. I say we go back ta the 'ouse, ta bed, and let 'is lordship do whut—''

"He is here," Lissa cut in, "I am certain of it."

"And 'ow can ye be so certain-sure, m'lady?''

"Because," said Lissa, eyes straining as she glanced upriver, "of the many things I learned about Lord Wylde last evening, I now know that a promise made by him is a promise kept." She squared her shoulders. "Come. He will be angling near the downed log, I am sure."

Tilly shivered, falling back into step behind her lady.

"Coo," whispered she, "but I be afeared of whut *else* m'lady learned from 'at man last night."

Lissa kept walking, not looking back, and making no reply to Tilly's statement. It would be best if *no one* knew what she had discovered while in Gabriel's arms last night. In fact, Lissa wished that she, herself, had no clue. Last night's happenings had changed her. Totally and forever.

For good or bad, Lissa had been thrust into being something more, something wholly strange and new to her—and it was all of Lord Wylde's doing. His touch had transported her out of the cocoon she'd built about herself following her father's death . . . and his kiss while they had stood at the front door of the manor had taken Lissa into a realm where she'd never dared to tread but had only dreamt about.

Even more than that, Gabriel had made Lissa yearn for more of him.

'Twas a dangerous thing, this yearning. Though Lissa had only intended to use Gabriel's blackened past to her advantage, he had whipped the tables round and queered her game. Where only yesterday she'd been thinking of her sketches and nature diary, Lissa was now contemplating far beyond those hobbies. Not only had Gabriel managed to rob her of her past times, but he'd robbed her of the safe, secure and serene future she'd envisioned for herself.

What a perfect pirate the man was proving to be!

Lissa worried over what his reaction would be upon seeing her this morning. Would he be surprised that she'd gotten out of bed a mere few hours after falling into it? Would he be angry? Bothersome? Frightening? *Anything* was possible. After all, she really did not know much about the man who was Gabriel Gordon. . . .

All of these thoughts were swarming through Lissa's mind when she finally spied him near the downed log she'd traversed and had nearly fallen off of due to her vertigo. Gabriel's dark head was bent as he tied a fly to his leader.

Lissa summoned her courage and kept moving. Tilly meekly followed. Within a few moments the two of them were striding near to Lord Wylde, but at the final moment Tilly stubbornly held back, choosing to sit atop a river rock and pretend to be busy with her lady's satchel.

Lissa continued walking.

Gabriel finally looked up, as though he'd felt her presence long before he'd heard her. His darkling eyes were a maze of emotions, though none of them fully bared.

"Good morning," he said.

"Good morning, my lord."

"I did not think you would come."

His statement nettled her. "Of course I came. We've made a pact, you and I. Irregardless of what you may believe of me, due to the rumors, I am not one to shirk the vows I have made."

A long moment of silence slipped past, time enough for Lissa to become uncomfortable. If she wasn't mistaken, Gabriel was growing just as uncomfortable.

She nodded toward the fly at the end of his leader. "A green-drake, m'lord?"

He nodded. "The very one you created. I thought I might test its mettle this morn."

That he'd even bothered to remember the lessons she'd schooled him in yesterday surprised Lissa—that he was using of all things a green-drake at this time of morning surprised her even more.

"It might do," she said.

"Might?" Gabriel sounded miffed.

"When I told you about the green-drake, I'd been thinking of angling during the late-morning hours. However, given the time of day just now, I believe you should affix something else to your leader. Say, a minnowlike fly."

Gabriel lowered his pole. "You mentioned nothing of minnows yesterday."

"Yesterday we were not angling this close to the dawning of the sun," she pointed out.

He frowned. "Nor did I think," he muttered, "we would be doing so today, given your penchant to entertain your guests to all hours of the night."

Lissa lifted her chin, daring him to utter Langford's name. "It was my friend's natal day. A celebration was in order."

"One that doubtless went on past midnight. Am I correct?"

"Had you stayed, you would know the answer to that," Lissa shot back, her ire stirring.

"Aye," he said, his own mood shading into black, "had I stayed, I *would* know. Since I did not, though, I know not. However, I can guess what transpired." He took a small knife from the pocket of his coat, savagely cut the green-drake from the leader, then looked up at her. "You danced with him into the wee hours, didn't you, Lissa?"

She stiffened, not willing to give an inch. "I grow weary of where this conversation is heading, my lord, and so—"

"Gabriel," he cut in. "You are to call me Gabriel."

Lissa pursed her lips, drawing in a huge breath. "And so," she finished with purpose, ignoring his command, "I propose we get to the task of honoring our pact."

"You mean hooking the trout that ate your locket."

"That—and . . . and sharing with you my knowledge of insects."

"Hmmm," he murmured. "I have given that a great deal of thought, and it seems to me, Lissa, that there is more to sharing about the insects of the Dove than there is to trying to catch your trout. In fact, there is the very real possibility that given I actually catch the fish you seek, you will be beholden to continue spending time with me in order to keep up your end of our bargain. I am wondering now if you are willing to spend more time with me than it takes to catch your fish."

"I had thought of that possibility," Lissa said slowly. "And the answer is yes, I—I am willing to give of my time."

He seemed oddly pleased with that answer. His eyes

darkened perceptively as he gazed at her. "Even in light of what transpired last night?"

Was he goading her? Or did he, just as she, enjoy their kiss good night at her front door. "Y—yes," she murmured, her cheeks warming beneath his scrutiny, "even in light of last evening."

"Good," he said. Turning, he nodded toward his angling basket situated alongside the river. "I have brought with me from my lodge all manner of hooks, feathers and string. You should be able to construct a minnowlike fly from the assortment."

"How very far-thinking of you."

"Yes," Gabriel agreed. "It seems, of late, I am forever thinking of the future."

Lissa felt a wave of pure heat wash through her. She quickly ignored it, then moved toward his basket, knelt down, opened the lid, and rummaged through its contents.

Gabriel moved beside her.

It proved difficult indeed for Lissa to keep her mind on the matter at hand, but she forced herself to do so. For the next half hour, she explained to Gabriel the exact things needed in creating a minnowlike fly. She hand tied a replica using the supplies he'd brought, then schooled him in the precise way of presenting it in the water for the trout.

From then on, their morning together became not one of underlying emotion so much as it evolved into a sharing of knowledge and thoughts. As the sun climbed high above the Dove, and Tilly on her far-off rock alternately dozed and contemplated the foliage near her, Lissa and Gabriel got down to the basics of fly angling.

Lissa created numerous flies, some representing exactly the flies flitting about the river and others a compilation of those flies. Gabriel, with his masterful casts, laid each and every one into the water.

By noon, Gabriel had caught three trout, but not the one Lissa sought. She hunkered down near his angling basket, intent on tying yet another creation, when she heard a squeal of delight come from the woodline beside them. She looked up.

A young boy, not more than six years old, came scurrying into their midst.

"Papa!" the boy cried, racing straight into Gabriel's arms.

Gabriel, a smile breaking wide on his handsome face, stooped down to catch the lad in a strong hold. "What are you about, son?" he asked, lifting the boy high, "and where is your governess?"

"She ish coming," the boy said, slurring his *S*'s in an endearing lisp.

Lissa looked back to the woods, seeing an older woman coming toward them. She was garbed in dark colors, and wore her brown hair in a severe knot at the back of her head.

"Do forgive us, my lord," said the woman, who cast a quick, apologetic glance at Lissa, "but Master Harry insisted we bring you a picnic lunch. Indeed, he said he had promised it to you, and that you had agreed."

"He did, did he?" asked Gabriel, smiling up into the face of the boy. He set the lad down, then chucked him under the chin. "What a famous idea, Harry. I had not even noticed it was the lunch hour." He placed his large hands atop the boy's shoulders, then gently turned him about in Lissa's direction. "Allow me to introduce you to Lady Lissa Lovington, Harry. She is our neighbor. Her estate marches with ours alongside the Dove." Gabriel looked up at Lissa. "I present to you my son, Harry."

Lissa looked into the very blue and precocious eyes of Master Harry and instantly fell in love. He was extremely handsome, with a shock of blond hair, eyes robin-egg blue, and a sweetly devilish glint about him. Where Gabriel was all darkness and exuded confusing emotions, Harry was a delightful opposite.

"How do you do?" she said, smiling.

Harry gave a proper bow, then curiously moved to Lissa's side, asking a number of questions about what she was doing with all the hooks and threads and feathers.

"I am constructing handmade flies for your papa to use while he angles. Would you like to help me?"

"Oh, yes!" said Harry. "I would like that very much!"

Lissa laughed. How refreshing was his honest exuberance. She motioned for Harry to settle down beside her. The boy did just that, and soon the two of them were huddling together and picking through all of the accoutrements Gabriel had brought from his river lodge.

The boy's governess—Miss Fabersham was her name, Lissa soon learned—seemed truly nervous about whether or not Lord Wylde would accept this invasion during his angling, but when Gabriel nodded his acquiescence, the woman relaxed. She then began unloading the picnic basket she'd brought from the house.

While Lissa and little Harry constructed several flies, Miss Fabersham spread out a checked square of linen, then laid out plates that she soon piled high with fried chicken, fruit, chunks of bread, pudding and bean snaps. A bottle of wine soon followed. Before Lissa knew what was happening, she, Harry and Lord Wylde settled down to a riverside feast. Even Tilly accepted a plate, her cheeks pinking when Miss Fabersham shooed away her offer of helping serve the meal.

Harry appeared especially delighted. He talked and talked, asking question after question, and telling Lissa that he liked the flies they had created and hoped they could create more.

"Can we, Lisha?" he asked, not quite able to pronounce her name, and totally forgetting to address her as "my lady."

Lissa smiled, truly liking the little boy. Though he had none of his father's coloring, he certainly had a way with *her*.

"Of course we can," she assured him. "And do you know, Master Harry, there are other things we can do alongside this river," she added, forgetting herself and getting caught up in the boy's excitement.

"Truly, Lisha?" he asked.

She nodded. "Do you know," she said, leaning closer to him, "there is a nest of birds very close to here that I'd like to show you some day. The nest is in a very old tree alongside this river. You would know it the minute you see it because the tree looks like an old troll with a tall head and seven arms on each side."

"Oooh," said Harry, "I would like to view such a tree! What kind of nest is it, Lady Lisha?"

"A cozy one," Lissa said, warming to her subject and loving the way Harry hung on her every word. "It is deep and safe, and it has at least three eggs in it every summer, *all* summer. And every baby bird hatches and learns to fly."

Harry snuggled next to her, eating a leg of chicken, contemplating all she'd told him.

"Will you take me there, Lisha?" he asked.

She looked at Gabriel, who was watching her and his son. Suddenly, Lissa's heart spilled out and over within her chest, so keen was Gabriel's gaze on hers. It was as though the two of them had bonded more during this picnic lunch than they had ever bonded thus far. And Harry was the reason.

"Yes," she murmured to the boy, "I shall show you the nest some day."

"Papa, too?" he asked.

She glanced at Gabriel, who had not taken his eyes from her. "Yes, your papa, too, if he would like."

"Oh, he would like it," Harry assured her. Then, tugging on her sleeve so that she lowered her head to his, Harry whispered, "I think he likes *you*, too, Lisha."

Lissa felt her heart leap even as her cheeks warmed with

a deep blush. She smiled at Harry, pulled back, then looked at Gabriel, wondering if he'd overheard his son's words.

If he had, he made no show it. He merely took a bite of chicken, his eyes taking in both his son and Lissa, who were caught together in a ray of sunlight.

Chapter 12

It was late afternoon by the time Lissa and Tilly headed back to Clivedon Manor. Lissa felt as though she was walking on clouds, so light was her mood. Her day alongside the river with Gabriel and young Harry had gone swimmingly, and even though they had not hooked the trout she sought, Lissa decided she had never enjoyed a more perfect day.

"Coo," said Tilly, walking a step behind her and daydreaming as usual, "I swears 'is lordship's boy looks not a whit like 'im. If ever there be two opposites, they be the ones, yes?"

Lissa frowned. " 'Tis none of our affair, Tilly," she said sharply. "And do remember, you are not to repeat anything you saw or heard this day, is that clear?"

"La, m'lady, I remember 'at right well! Me chaffer be mum, I swears!"

"Hmm," said Lissa, not at all convinced, "I've heard *that* before."

"It be true," insisted Tilly. "I be turnin' o'er a new leaf, so's ta speak, I do swear. From this day on I be the perfect maid fer m'lady. It be my vow.''

Lissa felt a smile twist her lips. Yet *another* vow. Betwixt her own, Lord Langford's and Lord Wylde's, her life, it seemed, was filling with vows! Now she must add her abigail's to the list.

"Instead of vowing such a thing to me, Tilly, please just live it and show me instead of telling me," Lissa requested.

With that, Lissa hurried inside, leaving Tilly in her wake to stare after her with a befuddled expression on her face.

Once inside, Lissa found many missives awaiting her. Though exhausted from her day by the river and from her near-sleepless night before that, she sank down onto her chair at her writing desk in the day room and began to read through the notes.

The first was from Lord Quinn, one of the many gentlemen who had arrived in the shire seeking to woo her. He had asked Lissa earlier in the week to join him for an outing of watching a balloon acension that was to take place on Thursday next. Though Lissa had not given him a firm answer, he now wrote to say he'd been summoned just this morning back to the Metropolis due to the illness of a dear aunt who was requesting his presence alongside her sickbed.

Lissa deduced Lord Quinn's hasty exit from the shire had more to do with Gabriel's presence last night than with any ailing aunt.

Ah, well, whatever the reason, she was now minus one suitor.

She broke the wax of the next missive. 'Twas from yet another suitor, and, amazingly enough, he too had been called back to London. Instead of an aunt having taken ill, this suitor claimed one of his thoroughbreds had injured a leg during an exercise session out of the mews and he must, by all means, hurry home to oversee the care of his most prized piece of cattle.

Lissa read the next missive, and the next, and so on. All heralded the same information; her suitors, one by one, were begging off! What had begun as an uncertain day had certainly become a perfect day, she decided.

By the time she read through the bulk of them, however, Lissa's good mood had but one cloud still to mar it—there was not yet a note from Lord Langford.

The door of the day room opened. Aunt Prudence stepped inside. *"Here* you are, my dear. I've searched the grounds for you the whole day long, I swear. Just now I spied your abigail, who told me you could no doubt be found at your writing desk. She's drawing a bath for you, said you'd as like be needing one, what with all the time you spent alongside the muddy river. Dare I ask with *whom* you spent your day near the river, my sweet?"

Lissa pushed away the missives she'd already read, reaching for the last one. "Ask away," she said, her voice sounding tired. "My guess is, you already know the answer."

"Do not say you spent the entire day in the presence of that blackguard, Lord Wylde!" Prudence was horrified.

Lissa ignored her aunt's dramatics. "Very well, I shan't say it."

Prudence pursed her lips. "As if his abominable behavior with you last night was not enough to set people talking, and your ridiculous notion of a pretend liaison to boot! Really, Lis, I do not like you being thrown into acquaintanceship with such a man."

"I am not being *thrown* anywhere, Aunt Pru. Kindly cease referring to me as though I am some scatterbrained chit fresh from the schoolroom."

"Faith, if only you *were,* perhaps then I could talk some sense into you. What possessed you to seek the man out after the vulgar scene he orchestrated last evening for all of your guests to view?"

"Lord Wylde was far from vulgar, Aunt Pru."

"What fustian! The man intended to sully your good name, and the both of us know it to be true! His intentions, when he held you and kissed you so boldly at the cusp of the terrace and the dance floor, were notorious indeed!"

"Very well," Lissa muttered, "if you must persist in knowing the truth, it is all because of a trout."

"A what?" Prudence asked, not at all understanding.

"I sought out his lordship this morning because of a trout," Lissa explained.

"You have quite befuddled me now, my sweet. What the deuce does some fish have to do with all of this?"

"Everything," Lissa said. "This particular trout ate a locket given to me by one Lord Roderick Langford—"

"Ah, Lord Langford! For once, my dear, you've uttered a name I can approve. Langford is of a good air and address. He should do nicely . . . that is, should you ever decide to come down to earth and begin thinking of marriage."

Lissa grimmaced, then continued, "Lord Langford affixed this locket about my neck, telling me the same would be our private sign to him of whether or not I will accept his suit. If I return the locket before the end of the Summer Season, then he will know I am not interested. If I do not . . . well, then, 'tis obvious what he will think."

Prudence failed to see the enormity of the situation. "Then simply let the locket rot, I say," she suggested. "You could do worse than the likes of Langford, Lis."

Lissa was not about to hash out her gut feelings about Langford—at least not with her marriage-minded aunt.

"I *must* have the locket back, Aunt Pru," she insisted. "It is imperative to me. I will not be cornered with the dangling of some locket in my face."

Prudence digested this information. "So, you went in search of Lord Wylde only because he may be helpful in retrieving this locket?"

"Yes," said Lissa.

"And for no other reason?"

Lissa bit her bottom lip.

Prudence eyed her closely. "Out with it, my sweet," she said.

"Very well . . . that isn't the whole of the matter. I *wanted* to see Lord Wylde this day, and to spend time with him. I—I should like to get to know the man he is, Aunt Pru."

"I dareswear his behavior last night was flag enough of the man's ways. I give you fair warning, Lissa, the man is not at all of your cut. During his salad days he sliced a swath through the finest of London's belles, and the poor woman he finally chose decided to end her life. Now I ask you, is that the sort of future you wish for? You would be far better off to choose one of the many other suitors who have come from the Metropolis in search of your hand in marriage."

Lissa, gnashing her teeth, was hard-pressed not to rally back at her aunt, but she knew Aunt Pru loved her and was only concerned about her virtue and her happiness.

Taking a deep breath, Lissa motioned with one hand toward the many missives she'd opened from the silver salver. "Witness these," she said.

Prudence turned her gaze to the many notes. "Invitations?" she asked, a hopeful note in her voice.

"Not by far, Aunt Pru. In fact, they are, all of them, notices that I am being given the rub off. From Lord Appleby to Baron Xavier, my suitors have begged off one by one, scurrying back to Town and forgetting their weeks of wooing me in Derbyshire."

Prudence's face fell. " 'Tis Wylde's doing," she breathed. "How I loathe the man!"

"You do not even know him, Aunt Pru. Please, do not prejudge him as so many others have. And pray, do not look so crestfallen on my account. I cannot tell you how relieved I am to have these missives."

"*Relieved?*"

"Yes. Don't you see? My plan of a pretend liaison is

working famously. I have rid myself of nearly all my suitors in one fell sweep."

"No, what you have done, my sweet, is begun a dangerous affair betwixt yourself and a man who has shown little care for those around him."

Lissa refused to listen to her aunt's words concerning Gabriel. "You cannot dash my good spirits, Aunt Pru, no matter what you say or think. I am glad, I tell you, to finally be given some room to breathe in my life. Nearly all of the gentlemen who have plagued me for so long have left the shire. There are only two who have not sent word to me. There is Chesney, but since he lives but a stone's throw away—"

"You can nix young Chesney from your list of suitors, Lis," Prudence interrupted.

"Oh?"

"Yes. Had you bothered to linger long enough to join us at the breakfast table, you would know that Chesney arrived this morning to escort Lavinia home."

"He *did?*" asked Lissa. She smiled at the thought.

"It seems he is suddenly quite enamored of our friend, always was, or so he whispered to me. He'd thought, given all of Vinnie's time spent cloistered at home with her books and her aged governess, that she was not interested in marriage, and so did not press his suit. Once they danced together and had time to themselves to talk, the two of them struck a chord."

"How wonderful," breathed Lissa, truly happy for her best friend. "I shall have to pay a visit to Vinnie and hear about all of this firsthand."

"She requested that you do just that. She was positively glowing when young Chesney led her to his carriage."

"I am sorry I was not here to see her off, or to say a proper goodbye. It is just that this drafted locket has me in high fidgets, Aunt Pru."

"Not to mention the presence of Lord Wylde," Prudence commented wisely.

Lissa blushed. "There is that," she admitted. She lifted her chin, her gaze meeting her aunt's shrewd one. "He is not at all what people believe him to be. Of that much I am certain."

"He dared to kiss you on the terrace, in full view of all your guests, Lis!"

"Only to aid my own foolish plot," Lissa quickly interjected.

"Was *that* his excuse?"

" 'Twas no excuse. I truly believe a part of him wanted to help me."

"And the *other* half of him?"

"I—I have not quite puzzled that out," Lissa answered truthfully. She clicked her tongue, shaking her head, unwilling to dissect what had happened between herself and Gabriel. She did not want to ruin the sweet glow set inside of her from the happenings of this day. She'd enjoyed her outing with Gabriel and Harry so very much that it seemed a shame to mar it with worries about what his lordship may or may not have intended last night.

The truth of the matter was that his bold kiss on the terrace last evening had been overshadowed by his sweet kiss at her doorstep and even more so by the lovely morning and afternoon she'd spent with him near the river.

"What matters to me most at the moment, Aunt Pru," Lissa said, "is that for the first time since ending the formal mourning for my father, I feel as if my life and my future have been returned to my own hands." Lissa reached for the very last, unopened note upon the salver. "A-ha," she exclaimed. "This final missive bears the seal of Lord Langford. Famous! I trust it is notice to me that he, for whatever reason, has found himself called back to the Metropolis. Once I open this, I shall be free to return to my old way of life."

Prudence did not appear convinced. "What about Lord Wylde? How will you extricate yourself from *his* pursuit?"

"He is not pursuing me," Lissa said, even as she broke

the wax of Langford's note. "The two of us are simply playing out our own portions of a certain vow."

"One that will doubtless have an unpleasant end for you, I fear."

Lissa, though, was barely listening to her aunt's dire prediction. Instead, she was amazed to read Lord Langford's bold script detailing his pleasure of dancing with her the night before. He ended the note stating that he was now more determined than ever to win Lissa's heart given the fact that Lord Wylde had entered the picture, that he would look for her wherever she tread in the shire, and that he could not wait for their planned picnic outing to take place on Monday next. He added, too, that he was glad she had yet to return his locket.

Lissa's heart fell. "What a disaster," she whispered.

"Do not say Langford has tucked tail and returned to Town as well?" Prudence said.

"Quite the contrary," Lissa replied solemnly. She looked up. "Lord Langford seems all the more intent on sewing up a marriage with me. He has promised to shadow my every step."

Prudence brightened. "Good. You would do well with reconsidering the man's offer."

"No, it is *not* good, Aunt Pru! Gabriel—er, Lord Wylde, has made the very same promise!" Lissa tossed down Lord Langford's note. She sat back in her chair, overcome by a deep-seated and fearful shudder. "Only imagine what will happen should Wylde and Langford come to blows over me. Oh, Aunt Pru, what I have done? What have I *begun?*"

"A pretend liaison, my dear, with not one man, but two."

Lissa felt like crying.

Prudence, the bangles about her wrists tinkling, put her arms about her niece. "Just say the word, my sweet, and I shall step in and stop all this nonsense. In fact, I shall see that your bags are packed and you are soon away from here. You can come back to Mayfair with me. Or we could go exploring somewhere far, far away."

"I do not wish to go away, Aunt Pru. I love this shire, the river, these lands . . . And mayhap," she whispered, her voice catching, "I—I might even love Lord Wylde."

Prudence held her tighter, saying nothing.

The next two days began exactly the same, with Lissa up before the dawn and hurrying to the Dove to meet Gabriel. Though they fished for their trout in earnest, they did not catch the thing. But together they tied numerous flies, and discussed the habits of trout, the beauty of the river, and the many wonders they found alongside the Dove.

In the late mornings, with little Harry in tow, they searched for nutes and cadis flies at the river's edge, then picked forget-me-nots.

On the third day, during the mid-afternoon after Harry had gone home with his governess and Lissa and Gabriel parted company, Lissa found herself filled with a restless energy. It seemed she'd been spending so much time with Gabriel that she'd forgotten how to occupy her own self! Not wanting to face up to the implications of that fact, she put on a fresh walking gown, pinned up her hair, then placed a straw bonnet atop her head. She decided she would walk to the rectory and leave a basket of baked goods.

She thought to take her nature journal along and perhaps jot down some observations. But the journal was not in her satchel. Had she forgotten it along the riverbank? She'd been in such high emotions over the past few days that she could not remember.

Not wanting to seek out Tilly, Lissa chose to go without her journal. She would simply brand every detail into her brain, she decided.

It was a perfect June day, sunny, the air filled with the

scent of flowers, and light, fluffy clouds dotting the sky.
Heading down the lane, with her ladened basket in hand,
she thought she might look for some moon daisies, and
perhaps keep an eye out for a painted lady butterfly.

But as she walked, a breeze rustling the ribbons of her
bonnet, it was not the nature surrounding her that she
thought about. 'Twas Gabriel. It seemed that everywhere
she looked, she saw a picture of him in her mind; his
smile so handsome, his dark eyes so seductive. She could
remember everything about him so clearly . . . the broad
expanse of his cheekbones, the huge breadth of his shoulders, the feel of his muscled arms about her. Oh, the feel
of those arms! So warm, protective, but frightening, too,
due to his sheer strength! She recalled his kisses most of
all . . . hot and demanding one minute, then soft and
beguiling the next.

She was amazed at the wanderings of her thoughts. Here
she was, only a few hours out of his presence, and she
could do naught but think of him, remember him, grow
warm inside at the images of him that played over and
over in her mind.

Heavens, she thought, with what would she fill her days
when the trout was caught and when Gabriel would have
no need of her tutelage in the art of creating handmade
flies? How empty her life would be then! It did not bear
thinking of, she knew.

Suddenly, there came the sound of hooves on the road
in front of her. She looked up, raising one hand to the
rim of her bonnet and straining to make out the figure
astride. Could it be Gabriel? *She hoped it was Gabriel.*

But would *he* have chosen white for the color of a horse?
Lissa could only envision *him* astride a black hunter, perhaps with white forefeet so that when he rode fast in the
night it would appear as though lightning were streaking
beneath him and his mount. Perhaps he had several cattle
he favored, white being the color of one.

Rider and mount drew closer, slowing as they

approached. Lissa stood at the side of the lane, folding her arms together beneath the handle of her basket.

"Good day, my lady," said the rider, removing his tall hat and sketching what passed for a bow as he sat in his saddle.

Lissa looked up into the very blue eyes of Lord Roderick Langford. Though her heart fell, she forced a polite smile. "Good afternoon, Lord Langford."

"I've come calling for you many days in a row, but somehow you are never to be found," he said.

"I often go off on my own to sketch, m'lord."

"I see no sketchbook in your hands now. Can I assume you will not mind my company this day since you are not about to sketch?"

Lissa wished to fob him off, but decided she need not be so rude. After all, he'd not bothered her overly much of late. "I am headed for the rectory. I've some preserves, several loaves of bread and some pudding. You may join me, if you wish."

"I do wish it, my lady." He jumped down off the saddle, reached to take the basket from her hands, then fell into step alongside her, his white mare complacently following behind at the reins.

They walked a few paces in silence. "You have not returned my locket. I am glad of that."

Lissa grew uncomfortable at mention of the locket. Here was her chance to simply own up to the fact she'd lost it, to tell the man she did not want his suit, and then be done with it all. But she couldn't bring herself to say the words. She wanted, instead, to be able to hand the locket back to him and with that deed give a final farewell to him. Somehow, just saying goodbye without returning his property did not sit well with her.

"Are—are you enjoying your summer in Derbyshire, m'lord?" she asked, deciding to let his mention of the locket pass.

"It has its moments." He tipped a grin at her, though

it paled in comparison to the rare smiles she'd seen upon Gabriel's lips. "Such as when I am near you," he added. "You've a loveliness unmatched by any other."

Gabriel had said something similar to her, and his words had transported her up into the stars. Hearing Langford's statement, however, only increased Lissa's feelings of discomfort. Drat, thought she, if the man was bent on continuing in this vein, she must let the whole truth be known to him this instant. Just hearing him talk to her in such a private way made her feel as though she was sullying all the quiet moments she'd spent at Gabriel's side near the Dove.

"There is something you should know about me, Lord Langford," she said, gathering her courage. "I—I am not of the mind to marry, and I do not at all wish for your—"

"Please, say no more. I have heard that you have no interest in marriage. I'd like to be the one to change your mind, m'lady. I am a patient fellow. I can wait."

"I fear you might have a long wait, sir."

"I do not mind. I have come to be quite taken with you, Lady Lissa. I think you know that."

"I do, however, I—"

"Hush," he insisted, his voice edged with something that sounded surprisingly like a threat. In the next instant, however, that hard edge was gone, and he spoke on a softer note. "Not now. Not here, Lady Lissa. Let us just walk and enjoy the sunshine, shall we? I'd rather not have my hopes dashed on such a beautiful day."

She felt nothing for the man other than guilt that she'd not yet returned his locket. Perhaps it was this guilt that pushed her to allow him to walk with her to the rectory.

Whatever the reason, she soon rued her decision, for as they neared the church Lissa saw Gabriel. He was standing a foot away from its front entrance, seemingly caught in thought as he stared up at the place with its weathered but beautiful stone and wood. He turned his dark head toward them, hearing their approach and the soft nicker of Langford's mare.

His black gaze took in the sight of Lissa and Langford, side by side. Even from such a far-off distance, Lissa could see the thunder clouds gathering on his dark brow, could see clearly that his hands became fists at his sides.

She felt suddenly, *ridiculously,* as though she was a married woman found rendezvousing with her lover. With guilt causing her heart to hammer in her chest, she tried to wordlessly convey to Gabriel with her eyes that what he was seeing was not what he thought it to be. She'd not gone from his company at the river to Langford's company on the road without nary a thought. She was *not* playing both men for fools, was not toying with their attendance, or even hoping the two might come to blows over her.

Gabriel, however, appeared to believe just that. There came to his black eyes a wave of rioting emotions, and his countenance became stormy. With a stiffness that could not be concealed, he turned toward them, then waited as they neared his side.

Langford seemed extraordinarily pleased by the turn of events. "Ho, Wylde," called he, "who'd have thought we would meet up with the likes of you, and in front of the doors to God's house, no less. Might you be pondering journeying inside, say to offer up a prayer for your soulless self?"

Lissa was appalled. She opened her mouth, intending to give Langford a tongue-lashing for his rudeness, but Gabriel spoke first.

"If any prayer is offered this day, it should be on *your* behalf, Langford. Of the demons who walk this earth, you are of the highest order."

"Not in Polite Society, I'm not."

"Those you label your peers have no inkling about the true fiend you are, Langford."

"A fiend, am I? Let us be clear as to who of the two of us is hiding from life and haunting the Dove." He motioned with just a nod of his bright-haired head. "Go back to your river lodge, Wylde. Go back into hiding where you belong."

Gabriel appeared as though he would like nothing better than to send a fist into Langford's smug, too-angelic face. He made a motion toward the man.

Lissa, fearing Gabriel would resort to fisticuffs, took that moment to step between them. "That is more than enough!"

Langford, pleased, smiled thinly at Gabriel. "You heard the lady. Now if you'll be so kind as to step aside and excuse us, we shall be on our—"

"The devil I will," Gabriel breathed. "I won't excuse you, Langford. In fact, I don't want you anywhere *near* the lady."

Lissa had lost all patience. Angered and appalled beyond belief, she took her basket out of Lord Langford's hands and glared at both men. "The two of you can take yourselves and this ridiculous conversation elsewhere. *I* am going into the church. *Alone.* When I come out, I pray both of you will be gone."

With that, she turned abruptly away—but not before meeting Gabriel's obsidian gaze and seeing his inner tumult mirrored there.

What was happening between the two of them? Were they merely honoring some hasty pact they had made . . . or were they headed for something more, something that was, until the moment they had met, beyond the reach of either of them?

Lissa didn't know. She knew only that she was angry and hurt by the foul words Gabriel and Lord Langford had shared.

She hurried inside the sanctuary of the church, glad enough when the door closed almost soundlessly behind her and she was enveloped in the vast peace of the holy place.

Chapter 13

Once inside, Lissa immediately moved to the side chapel and the little altar there. Behind it was an iron gate, and behind that were all the tombs of her ancestors, her parents included. She knelt down in front of the altar, setting her basket beside her, then bowed her head, hands clasped together, and prayed fervently that all the confusion in her life—and in her heart—would soon come to an end. She prayed for herself, for Gabriel, and even for Lord Langford. But she prayed most of all for Gabriel . . . prayed he would find some peace in his turbulent soul, prayed he might one day look at her without clenching that strong jaw of his and would see her as the friend she longed to be.

And a very daring part of her prayed that she and Gabriel might one day become more than just angling partners of the Dove . . . might actually come to love one another . . . to *marry*.

The moment the fervent prayer came whizzing through her mind, Lissa snapped her eyes open. She stared up at the gold cross atop the altar gleaming bright in a slanting of sunlight through the stained windows, and wondered at her own thoughts. Marriage, and to Gabriel! Imagine, she'd actually prayed for such a thing!

Lissa shivered, amazed that she was now on her knees in a place that felt like home and was praying mightily for a marriage with the sixth Earl of Wylde.

She hardly knew the man, she thought.

Then again, she felt as though she'd known his soul since the beginning of time. . . .

She heard footfalls in the adjoining passageway. She got to her feet just as the rector appeared. He smiled, obviously glad to see her.

"Good day to you, my lady," he said quietly. "I had been intending to pay a visit of late, but Widow Hawthorne took ill and I was needed at her bedside."

"I hope it is not life-threatening."

"She will recover."

Lissa nodded, smiled in relief, then motioned to the basket beside her. "I've brought some bread, preserves and pudding. I thought you and yours might enjoy them."

"Ah, we shall, my lady. Thank you."

Lissa smiled again, passing the basket to him.

"Is there something else?" he said, apropos of nothing, a sage note to his calming voice. "Something you wish to talk about, my lady?"

Lissa very nearly told all, but stopped just short of doing so. How to explain her own ridiculous plot of a pretend liaison, of all the hours she'd spent at Gabriel's side and how confused he made her feel. No doubt the rector would be scandalized to hear such things come from her lips. And how could she explain the two gentlemen outside who had very nearly come to blows over her . . . and, more to the point, how Gabriel could make her both happy and sad all in a single moment? No, she could not express all of this; it was for her own heart and mind to puzzle out.

Instead, Lissa said simply, "My—my life h-has been confusing of late."

"I am listening."

"I . . . I feel as though I am at a crossroads, that I could fall off into nothingness but at the same time as though I might actually come into something wholly wonderful and lasting." Lissa shook her head ruefully. "I am not making much sense, I fear."

"You are making perfect sense, and I am glad you came here this day, to pray. I blessed the union of your parents, my lady, baptized you, and watched you grow. I know that your mother and father schooled you well, and that you have been constant in your faith. Let that faith guide you now." He nodded toward the cross. "Take the time to seek the peace you know dwells within this house, and allow it to fill your own heart. Know that God will guide you, if you but ask."

Tears pricked Lissa's eyes. She swallowed, nodded, and whispered, "I will. I swear I will. Thank you."

Within a moment, the rector was gone, moving back into the shadows of the church, leaving Lissa alone, with her thoughts and her prayers.

She knelt once again, looked up at the cross that gleamed in a ray of slanted sunlight, and truly prayed for guidance.

Much later, as Lissa headed back outside, she was feeling renewed. She looked for Langford, his mount, but didn't see them. She blinked against the brightness of the sun . . . and then she saw Gabriel.

He'd lingered near the church, waiting for her. He stood alone on the gravel drive, arms akimbo, his gaze not as black as she remembered it a short time ago. He seemed to have calmed himself in the absence of Langford.

"I'd have thought you'd gone back to the river, or to home," Lissa said.

"You thought wrong." He offered her his left arm. "May I lead you home?"

"I am quite capable of finding my own way."

"Of course you are. But that's not why I asked. I asked because it would please me to do so." He again offered his arm. "May I?"

Lissa hesitated. "Your behavior with Lord Langford was atrocious."

"Aye. It was that."

"Have you no shame?"

"Where Langford is concerned? No, I don't. I never have, never will. Now, will you walk with me or not?"

"You have been insufferably rude this day."

"Not with you, I haven't." His eyes were tender, the heat of his anger with Langford gone. "Walk with me, Lissa," he said quietly. "Say you will. And tell me, please, what peace you found within the church."

"You need only go inside to discover that on your own, my lord."

"You are to call me Gabriel," he reminded her, and then, with a rueful grin when she made no answer, he glanced at the church, its doors. A long moment of silence slipped past, time in which he was clearly considering her suggestion to go inside.

"Ah, no . . . ," he finally said. "Not today. Not yet."

"Why?" Lissa asked quietly, hoping that he might truly open up to her and share whatever it was that tortured his soul.

" 'Tis a long tale, one I have not shared with any other."

"I am a good listener, m'lord."

"Aye," he agreed, "you are that." His lips turned with a deeper grin. "But you do not take direction well—as in my directive for you to address me as Gabriel."

Lissa frowned. "You are teasing me now. And here I'd thought the two of us might actually share something of import."

"No, what you thought was that *I* would do the sharing, and you the listening."

Lissa blew out an agitated breath. "You're insufferable,

my lord." She turned, moving briskly away, intending to walk home alone.

Gabriel, laughing, strolled beside her with infuriating ease. "I'll accompany you, if you don't mind."

"I do," she said crisply.

Gabriel ignored her remark. Lissa glanced at him out of the corner of her eye, and was amazed to see the lightness in his step, a grin still hovering on his too-handsome mouth. For the first time, it seemed, his guard had gone down, and she was being given a glimpse at the softer side of him. Even his black eyes held a bit of a smile in them.

"The change in you is this side of alarming, I dareswear, m'lord."

"Not too alarming, I hope." His grin lessened then. A serious note to his voice, he said, "I just . . . I'd like simply to walk you home, Lissa. We don't even have to talk. In fact, I'd rather we didn't. Truth be known, I've come to like our silent moments."

Lissa slowed her pace, the anger washing out of her. Amazingly enough, she knew exactly what Gabriel meant.

Gabriel walked her home, right up to her door, and they talked of nothing. They simply existed together beneath the sunshine.

It was, Lissa later decided, the finest walk she'd ever taken. . . .

During the next two days, Lissa's life became one of trying to dodge Lord Langford's presence and hoping for Gabriel's. While she spent every morning alongside the Dove with Gabriel and little Harry, she had her afternoons and evenings to worry over.

But even though she'd leave Gabriel's presence at the river, she came to expect him to crop up wherever she went. He seemed to materialize at any given moment as she came out of a shop in town or took a walk along the country lanes. But much to her consternation, Langford was often on the scene as well.

Several days after the unnerving scene between Langford, Gabriel and herself outside the church, Lissa decided to head into the village to the milliner's shop. She needed to purchase a new bonnet, one sturdy enough to endure her many ventures into the woods.

As was always her penchant, she chose to walk the distance, and was glad to be able to slip out of the manor without her abigail in tow. Truth be known, Lissa needed time to herself, to let all of her thoughts swirl in her head and, hopefully, settle down within her mind into some semblance of order.

The sun was blindingly bright, the air tinged with heady, summer scents, and the country lane was dusty and dry. Lissa simply allowed the sun to coat her, and the beauty of God's earth to wrap about her.

She reached the millinery by mid-afternoon, and allowed herself several minutes of mindlessly gazing into the clean window at the collection of bonnets on display. Though she'd come in search of a bonnet for walking, a stylish riding hat festooned with a plume of darkly dyed feathers caught her fancy. The feathers were a perfect match to Gabriel—to his eyes, his hair color, and mayhap even his darkling moods. . . .

Lissa bit her bottom lip, studying the hat, wondering at how she was of late forever equating anything and everything with thoughts of Gabriel. She knew she should stop such behavior—but, alas, could not. In fact, Lissa was suddenly thinking of how wonderfully the hat would complement her favorite charcoal riding habit come autumn, and was thinking, too, if she would be heralding in the fall season with Gabriel in her life. She hoped so.

Even in the face of the man's mercurial moods and the blackened rumors surrounding him, Lissa had several times glimpsed a pearl of perfect peace while in Gabriel's presence. Foolish or not, she harbored the hope that the two of them could together transcend all the angst that had thus far shattered those pearllike moments. Telling herself that what *seemed* impossible might actually *be* possible, Lissa headed for the door of the millinery, her spirits lifting.

The shop bell jangled above her as Lissa stepped inside.

Mrs. Emma Hodges, owner of the shop, a small, rotund woman of excellent humor, hurried forward to greet her. "Good afternoon, Lady Lovington," she said warmly.

Lissa smiled. "Hello, Mrs. Hodges. I see you've a new display in your window."

"Ah, yes, I can thank my new shop girl for that. She's quite handy, and good thing, too. I fear I'm getting too old, and too wide," she added with a wink, "to move myself around in such a small space. Anything in particular you like, m'lady?"

"There are several actually—and the riding hat most especially."

Mrs. Hodges beamed. "Excellent choice, m'lady. Though the black would be most striking on you, I can have one fashioned in the deepest shade of blue, if you prefer, or perhaps even violet, or—"

Lissa shook her head. "No, I like the black with its gray plumes," she said, thinking of Gabriel. "The one in your window is perfectly perfect, Mrs. Hodges. I'd like to purchase it. And I'd like to order a bonnet for walking, straw will do—one that is sturdy but pretty, with some sort of summery ribbon."

"Of course, m'lady," said Mrs. Hodges, quickly moving to the counter to make some notes. "I've always said you inherited your mother's beautiful face and form, and that any hat on you will look like a crown. How we miss your parents, m'lady. So in love with each other, they were, and so kind to all in the shire. I speak for myself and a good many other people, I dareswear, when I say I hope you, too, will one day enjoy such a perfect marriage match."

"Thank you," said Lissa, her cheeks suffusing with a soft

blush, for she could not help but think of Gabriel when the word "marriage" was uttered. It was not at all uncommon for those who dwelled in the shire to talk to Lissa in such a manner, no matter of their position. Her parents had been beloved throughout the village and beyond, and there had been a profound outpouring of love and sympathy at the passing of each of them. "I consider myself fortunate to be surrounded by people like you, Mrs. Hodges," Lissa said, meaning every word.

The woman smiled warmly as she completed Lissa's order. "I will have the riding hat delivered to you, m'lady, and will get right to work on your wish for a straw bonnet. You should have it in two days' time, less if possible."

"There is no hurry," Lissa assured her.

Mrs. Hodges placed the written order into a small wooden tray on her counter, then nodded toward the window. "Though you are in no hurry for your bonnet, m'lady, my guess is that the two gentlemen waiting for you outside are no doubt in a hurry for you to be finished with your business here."

"Two gentlemen?" Lissa said, then turned to peer out the shop window.

There, on the sun-splashed street stood not only Gabriel, but Lord Langford as well. They stood several feet apart, eyeing each other like two proud and territorial lion kings. Lissa frowned.

Mrs. Hodges, impervious to Lissa's sudden inner turmoil, hurried round the corner of the counter and opened the door for her. The bell jangled loudly. "Ah, to be young and sought after again," she said wistfully. "You've the world at your feet, m'lady."

At sight of Gabriel, who looked more brooding than ever, and Langford, who appeared as though he expected to be sole winner of a huge bet at White's, Lissa felt like she had nothing at her feet but a quagmire of male dominance.

"Thank you for your trouble, Mrs. Hodges," Lissa said.

"Thank *you,* m'lady, and good day to you."

Having no more business with the woman, Lissa reluctantly headed out to face the lone suitor who still plagued her, and the man who bore the name of an archangel and who had the sole ability to sweep her off her feet with just a look, just a caress. . . .

Once outside, Lissa blinked against the sunshine.

Langford reached her first.

"Greetings, Lady Lissa," he said, smiling broadly and tipping his hat, his hair bright in the sunshine. "Thought I'd accompany you home, if you like," he said.

"She *won't* like it," Gabriel cut in, nary giving Lissa a glance as he glowered at Lord Langford. "The lady will be joining *me* on her trek homeward, Langford, so you might as well leave and lick the wounds of your injured pride in private."

"*M'lord,*" Lissa gasped, spearing a heated gaze in Gabriel's direction, "really, *must* you be so—so *rude?*"

"Rudeness," said Gabriel, sidling beside Lissa and whispering into her ear, "is far too gentle a sentiment to even present to yonder cawker. Now tell me you will finally see the error of your ways and will turn your back on that cock o' the walk who clearly believes he has some say in your life."

Lissa blushed crimson, amazed that Gabriel could be so crass and in such a public place. And Lord Langford! Heavens, but he looked near fit to be tied, so incensed did he appear.

"Back off, Wylde," Langford threatened, his voice low and meant only for Gabriel's ears. But of course, due to the close proximity of Wylde's body to hers, Lissa heard every word Langford uttered to Gabriel.

She was suddenly thrown into a tailspin of emotions, and felt as though her privacy had been hideously invaded by their collective male egos. Becoming truly angry, Lissa backed away from Gabriel and Langford, lifted her chin, and glared daggers at the both of them.

"I will have you *both* know that I grow weary of your

very male demonstrations while in my presence," she said, surprising them both. "My wish is to walk home *alone,* is that clear? I am positively filled to the brim with the brutish behavior the both of you seem so bent on demonstrating!"

With that, Lissa marched off down the lane, determined to walk home in peace.

"My lady!" Langford begged, but Lissa would have none of his sorry apologies.

She kept walking. "Begone," she warned over one shoulder, "lest I decide never to see you again."

'Twas that very threat that forced Lord Langford to still his steps. With a muttered curse at himself and at Gabriel, he turned on his heel and walked away.

Gabriel, however, was not one to be so easily cast off. With determination, he set his paces in Lissa's direction, the devil be damned. He caught up with her just as she cleared the last lengths of the road inside the village.

Gone was any trace of his smile and the laughter he'd displayed near the church.

"I don't want you talking or even being seen with that cawker called Langford, do you hear?"

The day was exceptionally warm, and Lissa, in her day gown of sprigged muslin, was in no mood to hear ultimatums. "I do not like the tone of your voice, sir," she said. "Nor do I like your assumption that you can tell me with whom I can or cannot associate."

"Langford is a snake in the grass, can you not see that?"

"No," Lissa flared. "I cannot. And I take offense that you seem to view me as some untried chit who cannot make her own decisions. Begone, Lord Wylde, lest I truly get angry," she warned.

"Angry?" he replied. "Let me tell you about anger, Lissa. I taste it every time I see you near that man. I live it every time I envision you going so easily into his arms! The man is dangerous, Lissa, a fortune seeker. Hear me and heed my words, he will woo you until you marry him; then he will squander your inheritance and leave you alone in your marriage bed as he chases after some other pretty face. He will walk all over your heart and will not give a whit about your love."

Lissa was appalled. She wanted to slap Gabriel. She truly did! Did he actually think she was in love with Langford? What a ninny he was being! Couldn't he see that she loved *him*? That she spent every night dreaming about his touch, his kisses?

"You obviously haven't learned a thing about me," Lissa blasted at him. "*You* have been the perfect fiend where my heart is concerned, not Langford." The moment the words were out of her mouth, she wished she could snatch them back. Stifling a cry, she broke away and raced for home.

Gabriel followed. He caught one of her hands in his, gently spun her around, and then, without a warning, kissed her fully on the mouth. Kissed her so hard and so thoroughly, in fact, that Lissa's toes threatened to curl. When he was done, he lowered her by slow degrees back to the lane.

"Was that the kiss of a fiend, Lissa?" he whispered. "Was it the kiss of a man who would use you then cast you aside?" He stared at her long and hard. "Tell me," he demanded, "was it?"

Lissa, her lips pulsing with the remembered heat of his kiss, could only shake her head.

Gabriel let her go. "Remember the feel of my mouth on yours, Lissa. Remember that Langford, and not me, is the very devil in disguise."

With that, he took his leave, heading off into the line of trees, toward the river he could compass and know best, and back to his imposed life of exile.

Lissa stood atop the lane, her body trembling and her heart shattered by his sincerity.

"Oh, Gabriel . . . ," she whispered.

Why was it the two of them could not just simply say what was in their hearts. Why were they forever arguing?

* * *

That night, Gabriel decided to head to the Dove and finally end his vow with Lissa. He'd sworn to catch "their trout," and he would do just that!

Taking up his rod and his net, his basket and all the handmade flies Lissa had created, plus the Midnight Callers he'd constructed, Gabriel moved with purpose to the river.

It was the dark of the moon, and the going was treacherous what with all the brambles, fallen trees and undergrowth. And the insects—gad, what a swarm they created about him!

Gabriel pressed onward, though, soon coming to the lip of the river's edge. He extinguished his light, then set to the task of hooking that blasted trout. It took him three hours of solid angling before he even got a bite, then another hour after that before the old trout he sought surfaced to take the Midnight Caller.

Just as Lissa had told him, the trout proved to be a frenzied feeder. The fish nearly tore both body and hook from his line, so savage was its strike. Gabriel was forced to let out more line, then play the wild trout through the water. It gave him a devil of a time, trying to wind his line around the rocks and branches, and at the end it fought him magnificently.

He grew to almost regret having hooked the trout and then reeling it in. It seemed a huge pity to kill a creature that was so full of life and energy.

But when he'd beached the trout on the gravel—just as Lissa had schooled him to do—and he'd relit his lamp, Gabriel saw that the trout was not so full of life; in fact, it appeared that its fighting on the line had been its one last act. In the days since eating Lissa's locket the fish had been injured on its left side. The poor thing had been deeply scored by the claws of some animal—a raccoon, perhaps, or maybe even a bigger animal.

Whatever the beast, the wound was deep and lethal. The trout hadn't many more days left to it. Mayhap that was the reason it had raised to Gabriel's handmade fly.

The only thing left to do was to end the trout's obvious misery, Gabriel knew. With a locket in its stomach and a huge gash in its side, the fish didn't have long to live.

Gabriel kneeled down and made quick work of ending the ordeal. He moved his knife with sure strokes, and wonder of all wonders found himself whispering a prayer for not only the hapless trout, but Lissa and himself as well.

Moments later he had the locket Lissa had sought with such a vengeance. He cleaned it in the river, held it in his palm, then moved it into the light.

His stomach churned when he recognized the small family arms etched into the backside of the gold, heart-shaped piece.

"Langford," he breathed.

The locket bore the seal of none other than Roderick Langford! Lissa had had him angling for a locket obviously given to her by that foul fiend!

Bile rose in Gabriel's throat. What a fool he'd been. What a perfect, idiotic fool. . . .

Chapter 14

Lissa awoke to a disturbing revelation the next morning; she'd overslept!

"Oh!" she cried, throwing off her covers and hurrying out of bed. "Drat that Tilly for not waking me," she said, then cursed her own self for sleeping so late.

She yanked open the curtains, cringing when she saw how fully up was the sun. She raced to get dressed, wondering if Gabriel was at the river wondering if she'd chosen not to join them due to the words they had shared yesterday.

She was just about to ring for Tilly when her maid's knock came upon the door.

"There you are! It must be nearly eight o'clock, Tilly! How could you allow me to oversleep?"

Tilly's look was somber. She held a bundled package in her hands. "It be frum 'is lordship, m'lady. And the servant whut delivered it told me how Lor' Wylde be in one of 'is black moods all the night long and how 'e wuz gone frum midnight ta the wee hours, then banged about 'is house just afores 'e sent this package to ye, m'lady. He also sent word there be no need of anglin' this mornin'."

Lissa felt as though the wind had been knocked out of her. Her haste immediately vanished and was replaced by a dull thud in the pit of her stomach. She looked at the package; within it was ill news, to be certain, thought Lissa.

Her heart tightened with dread as she took the bundled package then moved toward her bed. She sat down, her hands shaking as she untied the twine. Inside the rough wrapping she found her blanket, her nature journal . . . and the locket.

Tilly sucked in a gasp. "Yer locket, m'lady!"

"*Langford's* locket," Lissa said, correcting her abigail.

"And there be a note—"

"Yes, Tilly, I see it," Lissa said, pure dread filling her. It would not be good news given the way he'd sent her belongings back to her. What had happened since yesterday? Certainly they had parted on a bad note . . . but she'd not thought their heated exchange would be a precursor to *this*. Was it just yesterday that Gabriel had kissed her so passionately? Now, holding his folded note in her trembling hands, that moment felt like an eternity ago.

"Are ye not curious 'bout the note, m'lady?" Tilly asked.

"Yes, of—of course I am. It is just that I . . . I need a moment to gather my courage before reading it."

Slowly, she opened the folded slip of paper. 'Twas not a long note. Not at all. He did not begin it with an address, or even end it with a closing. In his bold handwriting, Gabriel had written simply:

> *Your locket and your belongings. Our pact is now complete and finished.*

Lissa pressed her eyes shut against the tears she felt welling in them. Within her chest, her heart shattered into a thousand pieces.

"M'lady?" Tilly whispered.

Lissa did not respond. She couldn't. She felt as though her world had just bottomed out.

"I be afeared, m'lady. Ye look as how yer insides have just died."

"An apt description," Lissa finally said, lifting her lashes, tears spilling from her eyes.

She set down Gabriel's note and picked up Langford's locket. "What a perfect nuisance this locket has been for me," she said through her tears. "Why, look, Tilly, it isn't even painted. All this time I could have sworn it was a painted piece, but it is pure gold. Do you know, I never even truly looked at it? And I'd touched it only to try and open the clasp."

Tilly said nothing, clearly fearing her lady had gone mad.

Lissa turned the locket over in her palm. "Dear God," she breathed, "no wonder Gabriel is so angry. Look, Tilly, at the back of the locket. It bears the Langford seal. I'd never even noticed that fact . . . but I fear it was doubtless the first thing Lord Wylde noticed. I am only surprised he did not march into the manor and throw the thing back in my face."

Tilly was horrified by the mere thought. "Should I call fer yer aunt, m'lady, bein' 'at yer bound to be stewin' about Lor' Wylde's note and all?"

"Stewing?" Lissa repeated, her mind spinning with all that had just happened. "Yes, that was my first reaction, I fear . . . and the tears. But now that I think of it, I shall not sit in my rooms and try to bandage my heart. No. I shan't."

Lissa drew in a huge breath, dashed the wetness from her face, then got to her feet, the locket still clutched in one hand.

"I shall," she said, thinking aloud, "just have to talk to Lord Wylde about this. In fact, there are a good many things I wish to say to the man today. It takes two to make a pact, and this party is not yet finished with my end of our shared vow! I shall, once and for all, own up to my feelings and tell Lord Wylde that the unmarriagable Lady

Lissa has come to the conclusion that she *is* of the mind to marry and would like to do so with *him*."

"*M'lady!*" Tilly gasped.

Lissa turned toward her maid, a renewed light in her eyes. "Tilly," she said, suddenly taking charge of both her emotions and the situation, "bring me my writing utensils. I shall pen a missive to Lord Langford, informing him that I wish to meet with him this afternoon."

"Whut are ye goin' ta do, m'lady?"

"I am going to return the man's locket and see him out of my life forever."

"And as fer Lor' Wylde?" Tilly asked, afraid of the answer.

"I am going in search of him. Alone. Lord Wylde and I have much to discuss. Now hurry, Tilly, I've much to do this day!"

Less than an hour later, Lissa, dressed in a walking gown of moss green sarcenet and wearing a light cloak with the hood secured over her head to ward off the morning's chill, made her way alone to the river.

She was just about to the spot where the downed log lay when she heard a high-pitched and rather worrisome call from afar.

Looking up, Lissa saw Miss Fabersham, appearing much the worse for wear and with a knitted frown atop her brow. The woman appeared to be in great distress. Her half boots were muddied, as were the hems of her dull skirt, and her hair had fallen loose of its usual tight bun at the nape.

"Miss Fabersham!"

The woman waved, a cry catching in her throat. "My lady! How *glad* I am to see you!"

"What is it?" Lissa called.

"Master Harry . . . he—he is missing, my lady! He was not in his nursery this morning. I have looked *everywhere*. The stables, where the new kittens were born, in the kitch-

ens, everywhere he loves to go," she explained, a terrified
edge to her voice. "I thought perhaps he wandered near
the river."

Lissa was instantly galvanized into action. She noted a
sort of dam made by silt and rocks in a near bend of the
water, and then headed for it. In a moment she was across
the water and standing on the opposite bank with Miss
Fabersham.

"I do not know what to do," the governess said. "I fear
the worst. I have called an alarm. Even now, his lordship
and the servants are mounting a search for the boy. I—I
thought perhaps he'd remembered our picnic by the water.
I thought he might have come this way. You haven't seen
him, have you, my lady?"

"No, I haven't. But I've only just now arrived at the
river."

"Oh, my . . . ," worried Miss Fabersham.

"We shall find him," Lissa said. "Do not fret. He cannot
have gone far. Are you certain you checked every inch of
the house?"

"Quite certain . . . Oh, but he is so very curious," said
the governess, *"anything* could have taken his fancy. Perhaps he walked into town. Perhaps he followed some stray
animal. Anything is possible where Master Harry is concerned. I should have kept a better watch over him, should
have—"

"Let us not waste precious time with 'should have's,"
Lissa cut in. "We need to find him, as soon as possible."

"Yes, yes of course. But *how? Where?"*

The woman was panic-stricken. Lissa knew that she, herself, might soon be as well if she didn't move into action.
"I shall scout the area upstream," she said, thinking of all
the places she and Gabriel had fished with little Harry.
"You begin your search here and go downstream."

Miss Fabersham nodded.

"Where is Lord Wylde searching?"

"Nearest the road, m'lady, and the lands that march

with yours. The servants have fanned out in the woodlands, to the north, south, east and west."

"And your signal if anyone finds the boy?"

"We are to return home immediately with him and sound the warning bell three times, alerting everyone else to end their search."

Lissa digested this information, and then, wishing the governess good luck, she headed upstream, calling out for Harry as she went. There could be nothing heard in return but birdcalls and the unending flow of the river.

Lissa looked over at the Dove, shuddering to think that Harry, reaching for a fly casing or even a brightly colored rock, might have fallen into the river's waters. Fear and panic ripped through her at the possibility.

She pressed one hand to her mouth, willing herself to be calm, to not give in to the stark fear that threatened to overwhelm her. Anticipating the worst was not going to help Harry. Staying calm, being clear, was the only thing that would aid him.

Lissa took a deep breath, called out for Harry, then continued walking. *Where could he have wandered off to, where could he have gone?*

He liked the kittens in the barn, Lissa remembered, had told her about them in great detail. But Gabriel and the others had doubtless searched that area high and low. What else was the boy taken with, fond of, intrigued by?

Lissa paused, trying to think hard, to remember exactly everything she and Harry had talked about. But it was the river that kept catching her gaze. Sunlight sparkled atop it, its light looking like a silver sheen. The trees on the other bank were tall, serene . . . the riverbank a deep blue-black. Lissa stared at those trees, willing her mind to think like a child's mind—like Harry's mind. What would draw him out of his bed and out of the house? What treasures might he seek?

Something rustled in the woods behind her. Lissa, far too on edge, swung about. A turkey cascaded in the air down from its previous perch on a tree limb, feathers ruffling as it dropped to the ground and scurried forward a few paces. One lone feather floated off its body, drifting on the breeze for a split second, then floated in a whispering, willy-nilly path to the forest floor.

Lissa stared at that feather. And then she remembered with startling clarity: *The tree, that looks like a troll. . . .*

The nest! She'd told Harry about a certain nest that all summer long would hold eggs that hatched into birds, told him about the mother bird who seemed able to produce eggs numerous times.

Could he have gone to look in on the fledglings? It was possible. At the moment, it was her only hope.

Lissa's feet suddenly flew over the ground as she raced upstream. She ran as though her life—and Harry's—depended upon it. That nest was too close to the water, and far too high up in the tree for little Harry to get to safely.

There were countless tragedies that could befall the boy should he attempt to climb that aged, dying tree on his own. And the nest itself had been built too far out atop a most precarious limb.

"Oh, Harry," Lissa gasped aloud, swiping away her tears as she did so.

If he'd gone to the find the nest, if he was hurt—or worse—because of his dangerous adventure, she would never forgive herself.

Lissa ran until her lungs burned and her head felt dizzy. She was still yards away from the tree, though.

"Harry!" she called out. "Harry, are you here? Answer me, please!" She was nearly to the tree when she heard a muffled call. "Harry? Is that you?"

She heard nothing . . . and then: "Lisha?"

She nearly hit the trunk of the tree headlong, so fast was she running. She pulled to a stop, cranking her head back and looking up. "Harry? Are you up there, sweetheart?"

"Lisha, look! I found the nesht, *nest,*" he corrected. "It is jush—just where you said it would be."

She could see him now—or rather, could partly see him. He was hidden by the leaves and crooked branches.

"Oh, Harry," Lissa breathed, relief flooding through her at the sound of his voice. "How did you climb so high in that tree?"

"I dunno," said the boy. "I just did. *Look,*" he insisted again. "Three babies, Lisha. Newly hatched. You were right, Lisha. What a special nest it is!"

"Oh, sweetheart. Please, hold still. Do not budge an inch."

Lissa moved to get a better view, seeing that Harry had climbed far out onto an aged, creaky branch, one that was positioned directly above a deep pool of water below. He was clinging to the branch with both hands and the strength of his little legs.

"I've been watching them," Harry called down. "They cry a lot. Do you think they are crying for their mother, Lisha?"

Lissa forced down an overwhelming sense of panic. "No doubt they are just hungry," she called back. "Now listen to me very carefully, Harry, I want you to—"

"Can I feed them?" he asked, his mind still on the birds, oblivious to the danger he was in.

"No, Harry, we should not disturb them. They are creatures of nature and we need to let them be. And I need *you* to come down out of the tree now. Everyone is very worried about you. We need to get you home and let your papa know you are safe. Do you hear, sweetheart?"

But Harry was already inching forward on the branch, his interest in the nest outweighing all other factors.

Wood creaked, and then, suddenly, the old branch gave an inch or two, threatening to split from the tree, jarring the boy as it tipped downward several inches.

Lissa's heart caught in her throat. *"Harry."*

"I—I'm okay, Lisha."

"Harry, *please* listen to me and do only as I say. You need to come down out of the tree, *now*. Just scoot backwards very slowly and—"

"I—I can't. I . . . I am afraid, Lisha." His voice rose a note as he clung to the branch. "Will you come and get me, Lisha. Please?"

Lissa looked up at how high he'd climbed. 'Twas frightfully high. Impossibly high.

"I want to come down now," he called. "I—I want to be with you, Lisha. And Papa."

"Oh, Harry," she breathed. She wanted to climb up and help him, she truly did. But he was so very high up in the tree. Just thinking of how far up he was made Lissa's stomach clench.

Did she have enough time to run and find Gabriel? Even as Lissa thought of that avenue, she nixed the idea. She wouldn't—couldn't—leave Harry alone in the tree. 'Twould be madness to do so. And yet . . . if she didn't, that left only one other plan; she must climb the tree herself and save the boy.

Lissa looked up, and up and up, at Harry teetering precariously on the old limb that was threatening to give way. There really was no choice at all in the matter. She *knew* what she had to do.

Lissa took a huge, deep breath of calming air, gathering not only her strength but her courage as well. She'd come to love the boy. Loved him so much that it hurt.

Tears in her eyes, Lissa called up, "I am coming, sweetheart. I'll get you down."

Before she even dared to think of what she was actually doing, Lissa reached up, grasped onto the lowest branch, then hoisted her body up and onto it. Her skirts proved a hindrance. She yanked them into place over the branch, then stood up, balancing precariously. Her half boots were slippery on the old, knotted wood. She forced herself to hold steady, to not panic.

Averting her eyes from the ground below, Lissa reached for the next branch, then hauled herself up again.

"Lisha?"

"Yes, Harry?" she asked as she climbed. She could no longer see him. She was climbing close to the trunk, where the limbs were strongest. Harry was hidden by branches and leaves.

"I was up early this morning. I—I heard my papa. I think you made him sad. Did you, Lisha? Make him sad?"

"Oh, Harry," she whispered, pausing in her climb. She was shaking now. She was too high up in the tree. So very, very high. She stared at the wood above her, forcing herself to stay calm. "I—I am going to share a secret with you, Harry."

Lissa climbed to the next limb, and then the next. "I would never do anything to make your father sad, Harry. Not intentionally. I've become quite fond of him. In fact, I . . . I have come to love the both of you. Very much."

There was silence then, interrupted only by the creaking of the tree and the ever-present rush of the river. "Harry, are you listening, sweetheart?"

"Yes," he whispered. "I love you, too, Lisha."

It was then she heard the soft muffle of his cries.

"Sweetheart, don't cry. Please don't cry."

"I am happy, Lisha. Happy that you came to save me, and that you love my papa and me. I think he loves you, too."

Lissa reached for the next limb, her own tears smarting her eyes. Harry did not know about Gabriel's note, that his pact with her was at an end.

"Lisha? Are you still there?"

"Yes, sweetheart. I won't leave until I have you in my arms. That's a promise."

"Oh," he said, sounding relieved. "Can we keep talking? I am not so scared when I hear your voice."

"Yes, of course, Harry. We shall keep talking the whole time, if you like." Lissa squeezed into a narrow space of limbs, hauling herself up yet again. "What would you like to talk about, Harry? The birds?"

"No. My papa."

"He loves you very much, you know. Even now he is searching for you."

"He told me yesterday that he had to save you from someone. Like a knight of old."

"He said that?" Lissa thought of yesterday's scene with Gabriel and Langford . . . of Gabriel's heated kiss. "After today, Harry," she said, "there will be no more need for your papa to save me from a certain someone. Today, at precisely three o'clock, actually, I will say goodbye to this someone, and your papa, I think, will be glad about that." Lissa knew she was rambling, and was perhaps saying far too much to a young boy who had no clear idea of what she was nattering about. But Harry wished to hear her voice, and so she'd just let the words come.

"I cannot wait for the afternoon, then," said Harry.

Finally, Lissa reached the spot where Harry teetered far out on the shaky limb.

"Hello, Harry," she whispered, at last able to see him fully. He was trembling, clutching the limb with all his strength.

"Have you climbed many trees, Lisha? I did not know a lady could climb a tree."

Lissa let out a shaky laugh. "I've never climbed a tree, Harry, until now. And only for you did I climb this one."

Far below her, Lissa caught a view of the river, its depths beneath the tree looking dark and ominous. Her laugh of a second ago caught sharply in her throat. She felt instantly dizzy and sick, the age-old malady of vertigo gripping her. There came the familiar panic in her breast, the roar of blood in her ears, and the pinpoints of light in front of her eyes.

Lissa clutched at a handhold, pressing her body back against the trunk of the tree and sucking in huge gasps of air. *Dear Lord,* she thought, *do not let me get sick here in this tree. Not now.*

"Lisha? You look scared, Lisha."

Lissa forced her eyes open. She willed herself not to look down, not to completely crumble with paralyzing fear.

"I—I am fine, Harry," she said, her voice no louder than a whisper. It seemed her vocal chords had shrunk. Stark terror was gripping every organ in her body now. "I—I need for you to come to *me,* Harry, f—for you to shimmy back on the branch, toward me. I'll reach for you. I'll grab hold of you. I promise."

The boy frowned, looking back at her over one shoulder. "Can't," he said. "I—I'm too scared, Lisha. Please help me."

Lissa's stomach threatened to revolt. She felt pinned to her spot . . . and yet, how could she leave Harry out on that limb, alone and terrified?

She took another gulp of air, blinking hard, pushing past her fear, and then, with one huge leap of faith she moved away from the trunk of the tree and eased her way out onto the branch.

"When I reach you, Harry," she said, "I want you to turn about and then throw your arms around me and hang on tight. Do you hear?"

Harry nodded.

Lissa inched closer. She was teetering on the aged branch, grasping nothing but the branch itself.

She felt it sag with her weight.

"Now, Harry. *Turn now.*"

He did, whipping his small body around and throwing himself against her chest. Lissa, mouth gaping wide in sheer terror, wrapped one arm about him and held tightly to the branch with her other hand.

The force of his slight weight was just enough to unbalance her.

Lissa swayed to one side, nearly toppling, then forced herself to simply trust that she could overcome her vertigo, the slim branch, and all the odds that mounted against them.

By slow degrees her body reclaimed its balance, and then, bit by bit, Lissa inched herself and little Harry back toward the trunk of the tree.

Just as she did so, the branch gave a hideous *crack* of sound, buckling beneath their weight.

Lissa, Harry clinging to her, fell five feet, crashing into another branch beneath them. She felt the whip of leaves in her face, the sting of short twigs scraping at her cheeks. But the sting in her right hand was worst of all. She'd clung to the branch until it snaked out from beneath them, and as they fell the skin from her hand was dragged over the length of the aged branch.

Lissa gasped.

Harry, his arms wrapped tightly about her neck, buried his face against her left shoulder and let out a scream.

It seemed to Lissa that his scream rent the very air.

We're going to die, she thought, her left arm burning from holding so tightly to the boy. *We're going to crash through these hideous branches . . . down into the deep depths of the Dove . . . and there is nothing I can do.*

Lissa thought of Gabriel then. Of how much he loved his son. Such thoughts were the last Lissa had as she and Harry plummeted downward. . . .

Chapter 15

Gabriel, looking for his son, scouted the area near the river hut and frowned mightily as that too proved unproductive. Where *was* the boy?

He shot out the door, racing for the river's edge and cursing himself and the boy's governess for not keeping a better eye on the precocious lad. Harry had always been given to moods of fitfulness. Perhaps it was because of the unpredictable infancy he'd endured; mayhap it was due to his heritage on his mother's side. Gabriel had no idea.

But he did know that Jenny had been given to acts of outrageousness. She'd also been prone to dizzying highs and abject lows. Her mood could never be compassed. She was either giddily alight or was cast into a deep, emotional abyss. The woman's moods had changed so frequently that even Gabriel, who had been exceedingly patient with her, had been hard-pressed to even understand her.

Could Harry have inherited his mother's wild emotions? Was the boy's disappearance now a result of those riotous feelings? Gabriel hoped not. He would hate for Harry to have been bequeathed the very things in his mother that

Jenny had so despised. She'd hated her mercurial moods, and had warred against them all of her young and tragic life. She had loved Gabriel one moment and then hated him in the next. In fact, she'd been the perfect victim for the fortune-hungry Langford. She'd become so much pap in Langford's unfeeling hands. Gabriel choked on bile just thinking of how Langford had wooed Jenny only because of her fortune, then had cut all ties with her once he realized Jenny's father was in dun territory due to his sickness for gambling.

Gabriel forced the ugly past from his mind, racing away from the lodge and calling out for Harry. He racked his brain, trying to remember every bit of every moment of the recent past—anything that might aid him in knowing where Harry might have wandered.

It was then he thought of their picnic lunch alongside the river with Lissa. She had told Harry of a nest she'd found, of the eggs that were nestled deep inside of it. Harry had been mesmerized by the story.

Thinking of that moment, Gabriel headed upstream, toward the old, ugly tree that spread its branches out and over the deepest parts of the Dove River. He prayed that tree wasn't where Harry had gone. . . .

Gabriel heard a crash of limbs and the scream of his son just as he came to the base of the tree.

"Dear God! *Harry!*" he cried, and in a second he hoisted his body up and off the ground, grabbing for a stout limb. "Harry? Speak to me, son!" Gabriel yelled, trying to see up into the boughs of the tree. It was blastedly dark within the branches, and there were so many twisting, old limbs he could not see the entire way up.

"We are here, Papa. Lisha and me. A limb caught us."

"Lissa's with you?" Gabriel called, climbing still. He was climbing so fast and so furiously that the leafy branches were snapping in his face, cutting his skin. He cared not.

"We are here, Gabriel."

It seemed to Gabriel that her voice came to him straight out of heaven, so sweet and welcome was its sound.

"I—I can see the top of your head," she continued, a disembodied voice within the darkness of the old tree, but one that pumped comfort into his soul. She was above him, somewhere, holding Harry safe.

"If you turn your face—yes, that's it," she said, "and look up, to your right . . ."

Gabriel did, and then he saw her. Just as he'd imagined, his son was tucked securely in her arms. Her hair was in disarray. There was a slight trickle of blood from a scratch on her left cheek.

"Dearest God," Gabriel breathed. "You are not hurt, are you, either of you?"

Lissa carefully shook her head, as though she feared any huge movement would send them falling again. "No broken bones, I believe."

"Lisha came to save me, Papa. She climbed all the way to the top of the tree. Just for me."

"She is very brave," Gabriel said, hoisting himself up to the limb just beneath them, "considering her fear of heights." From his point on the lower limb, Gabriel's face was adjacent to Lissa's. Without even thinking, he lifted one hand and brushed a twig from her hair, smoothing a haphazard lock off her brow. "If you hold very still, I'll take Harry from you, climb down, and then come back for you."

"For once, m'lord, I do believe I shall listen to your directive."

Gabriel reached up, capturing Harry's little body in his arms, then sliding him down off Lissa's lap. The boy clung to his father, holding tight as Gabriel climbed down limb by limb. Once on the ground, he hugged his son close, placed a solid kiss to the top of his head, then climbed back up for Lissa.

She'd managed to climb down to the limb he'd just

vacated. "Here, allow me to help you, m'lady." Gently, he took her hand in his, the two of them backing down out of the tree together.

"You have a very curious and adventurous son, m'lord," she said as they drew closer to the ground.

"And it appears he has a very true friend in you. Thank you, Lissa. You saved his life this day, of that I am certain."

Once on the ground, the three of them moved quickly out from under the shadow of the tree. Harry appeared fearful that he would soon suffer a tongue lashing for spiriting away, but Gabriel only scooped the boy up in his arms, pressing his face into Harry's blond curls.

"I am sorry, Papa, but I wanted to see the nesht . . . *nest.*"

"Ssh," said Gabriel. "We will talk later about what lesson you should have learned from your adventure. For now, we must escort Lady Lissa home and—"

"No," Lissa interrupted. "I shall find my own way home. I insist. You must hurry back to your own house and sound the alarm so that your servants and Miss Fabersham can know Harry is safe. Besides, there is something I must do this day," she said, reaching out to run one hand against Harry's cheek.

Harry grinned at her.

Gabriel wondered what was going on, clearly some secret betwixt his son and the woman who had haunted his dreams since he'd met her.

"Go," Lissa insisted. "And please, Gabriel, do send word to me of a time when we can meet and . . . and discuss the note that was delivered to me this morning. I've something to say about this pact between us that you say is finished and complete."

With that, Lissa smiled at Harry, then turned and headed for home. Gabriel was of the mind to trail after her, but something in her words warned him she would not be gainsaid this day. And something in her voice, and the way she looked at him, told Gabriel she was going to have a good deal to say to him—not all of it bad—once they had their meeting.

"Now what was all that about?" Gabriel wondered aloud, cocking one dark brow at his son.

Harry shrugged his shoulders, grinned, then snuggled against him. "I am glad we live here beside Lady Lisha," he said. "And, Papa, I promise never again to climb a tree by myself."

Gabriel shook his head, his heart spilling over with love for his son . . . and for another person, a certain lady who dared to face her own fear of heights to save his boy.

He turned toward the path leading homeward, and as he walked, it suddenly occurred to him that Lissa had finally used his Christian name.

Chapter 16

Lord Langford arrived precisely at three o'clock. He was dressed superbly in a perfectly cut mulberry coat and cream-corduroy breeches, with a tall-crowned beaver hat atop his blond hair. He swept the hat from his head, bowing deeply before Lissa after being announced.

"I was so very pleased to get your missive," he said.

"Thank you for coming. I have something that belongs to you and would like—"

"Ah . . . my locket." His face fell.

Lissa steeled her resolve, knowing she had to do this as quickly as possible. She reached into the pocket of her skirt and withdrew the locket.

Langford frowned. "I shan't take it. Not yet."

"My lord, there is really no point in prolonging this. And though I hate to be the one to dash your hopes, I—"

"My lady, please, allow me a moment, if you will." He led her to her front door, opened it, then showed her his carriage that was on the drive. "I should like to show you something before we part company. I know you have asked me here today to bid me a final farewell. Given that, I wonder if you would be so kind as to come with me in my carriage. Before I take back the locket, there is something you *must* see."

Lissa hesitated. She did not want to go anywhere with the man. At any moment, word could come from Gabriel that he was ready for their meeting. She wanted to be at the ready for him. In fact, after her ordeal in the tree, she had hurried home to a hot bath, then had changed into a fresh gown—one of her best. She had chosen a walking gown of pink-spotted white muslin, and a brown spencer, and had carefully arranged her hair. Even now, her straw bonnet with its satin brown ribbons rested on the table near the door. When Gabriel sent word, she would be out of the house in a moment.

"I cannot imagine what you wish for me to see, and truly, I will still, at the end of our ride, return your locket."

"Please," said Lord Langford. "It is but a small thing I ask, is it not?"

Lissa realized he wouldn't end his press until she relented. "Very well, then. A short drive, mind you. It shouldn't take long, should it, to view this thing you wish me to see?"

Langford shook his head.

Lissa reached for her hat, then allowed Langford to lead her out to his landau and chestnut team.

They had gotten no farther than the end of the long drive, the hearty and well-matched chestnuts picking up speed, when Lissa espied a small, tow-headed figure dashing into their path.

"My lord, *take care!*" she gasped.

"Eh?" Langford said, confused by Lissa's outburst. And then, thankfully, he too saw the small boy rushing foolishly into their path. He hauled hard on the leathers, causing his spirited cattle, their iron-shod hooves sparking, to plow to a sudden halt. "Damnation," he groused. "What the devil—?"

" 'Tis young Harry, my lord. Heavens, what was he thinking?"

"Obviously the lad wasn't thinking at all. He nearly was cut down. I say, my lady, whoever is in charge of the little baggage ought to have his ears boxed for allowing—"

But Lissa wasn't listening. As soon as the carriage stopped she jumped down to the gravel, not giving a moment's notice to the height or even to her own ungraceful exit from the conveyance. Her thoughts were solely on Harry. She ran past the horses, straight for the child, whom she took by both shoulders and then scurried to the side of the drive, away from the now nervous chestnuts and their dangerous equine feet.

"Harry, what *ever* are you about?" Lissa demanded. "You should be home with your father! You could have been trampled, could have been—"

"I came to save you, Lisha, just like you saved me this morning," he cut in. He thumbed in Lord Langford's direction.

His lordship had dropped down from his seat to check on his horses. Now that he'd seen Lissa had the boy in tow, he stroked the horses' velvety muzzles, murmuring soothing words.

"Harry, you are proving to be a perfect nuisance this day," she said, then clicked her tongue, knowing she could never be angry with the boy. She instead hugged him tight, then held him back at arm's length, and said, "We will drive you home so that your father doesn't call another alarm, do you hear?"

Harry nodded.

Lord Langford came beside them then, his face livid with fury. "Of all the addlepated, hair-brained—"

Lissa instantly rose to her feet, turning to Langford. "My lord, *please,*" she said, interrupting his tirade, "I will ask that you keep your anger in check. The boy is a friend of mine."

"A *friend?*" said Langford, glaring down at Harry.

"Yes," said Lissa, moving closer to the boy. "A very dear one at that."

Langford, though not at all pleased by what had just happened—and clearly wanting to throttle Harry for the fright caused to his team—had sense enough to school his emotions to a calmer keel. "Forgive me, my lady," he said. "Any friend of yours will surely be one of mine. But I will admit the boy gave me a bit of a fright."

"As he did all of us," agreed Lissa, shooting a stern but loving look at Harry.

He smiled up at her.

"He is not harmed in any way, is he?" asked Langford.

"No," Lissa assured him, "thanks to your quick thinking, sir. But he *is* in need of a ride home. In fact, his family property is not far from us. You will not mind if he joins us for a short length, will you?"

Langford, though he tried to conceal it, did indeed mind. "No, of course not," he said. Langford glared down at Harry, whose blue eyes were very much like his own.

Lissa, not liking the tone Langford had taken, took Harry by the hand. She headed with purpose for the carriage, young Harry beside her.

Langford, realizing he'd made an error in speaking so gruffly about the boy, hurried to catch up. He let down the step, helped the boy and then Lissa to alight, then shoved the step back in place.

"I think he's mad," whispered Harry to Lissa as Lord Langford strode once more to his horses and checked not only their reins but their moods.

"He is not angry," Lissa whispered back, "only upset by your shenanigans."

Harry frowned. "I didn't mean mad like angry, but mad as, y'know, 'touched.' " Harry made a little curlycue with the fingers of his right hand beside his temple. "Bedlam-mad, Lisha."

"That is quite enough, young man. Now do sit still, and *behave.*"

Harry squirmed on the seat. "I came to be your chaperone, Lisha. Papa don't want you alone with the man. I don't either."

Lissa's heart did a queer flip-flop in her chest with Harry's words. She would have hugged the boy to her chest and told him that she had no designs to be with Lord Langford for longer than it took to still his suit and see him gone. She would have jumped down out of the carriage and raced Harry back to Gabriel if she could. But Langford was now heading back toward them. She didn't dare say what was truly in her heart. Instead, she said, *"Doesn't,* Harry. The correct word is *doesn't;* your father *doesn't* like me being near Lord Langford."

Harry nodded eagerly. "You're right, Lisha. He don't like it." The boy sat back, folding his arms about his chest and beaming, obviously mighty glad he and Lissa understood each other.

Lissa, unable to help herself, smiled lovingly at the boy. Langford finally climbed atop the seat beside them, took up the leathers and then clicked the chestnuts into motion.

A few minutes of terse silence followed as they cleared the last of the drive and then made for the open country road.

Harry seemed pleased enough with just sitting back and swinging his legs forward and back, given his feet did not yet reach the floor beneath him. Lord Langford, Lissa noted, was clearly irritated by the boy's restless nature.

"You gave us quite a scare back there, lad," Langford finally said. "You should never be so foolish again. I pray your family will give you a good talking to. If *I* were your father, I would see you had no lunch at all and were sent straight to your rooms for pulling such a prank."

Lissa was just about to verbally come to Harry's aid when the boy, with all the brashness of a six-year-old, piped up and said, quite clearly, "Then glad I am *you* are not my papa, sir."

Langford frowned, studying the road before them with more intent than was necessary.

Lissa, though she knew Harry should not be speaking to his lordship with such a brazen attitude, could not help but feel no animosity whatsoever toward the boy. After all, Harry had dashed in front of the carriage because he was worried about her and was attempting to be her white knight, her corsair. He'd taken it upon himself to come to her aid, and had also played a perfect Cupid betwixt herself and his father. Lissa felt herself melt a thousand times over just thinking about it all.

Langford handled the reins with undue force. "Just give the word, my lady," said he, "when we are to turn off for the boy's property."

By the tone of his voice that moment could not come soon enough. Lissa wondered what would be Langford's reaction when she directed him onto Gabriel's long drive.

That moment came all too quickly, it seemed.

"The turn is just beyond this bend in the road, my lord. You'll see the gates."

Langford's nostrils thinned. *"B'god,"* he muttered, having cleared the bend and seeing the gateway to Wylde's property. "You mean he lives on *Wylde's* property?"

Lissa braced herself. "Meet the Honorable Harry Gordon, son of the sixth Earl of Wylde, my lord."

Langford gaped at her. " 'Tis *his* son?" demanded his lordship, as though Harry was both deaf and dumb.

"Sir, *please,"* Lissa admonished. "Just turn to the right. I will see Harry safely to his doorstep. No doubt his father is beside himself with worry."

"No doubt," sneered Langford, "and yet the man is nowhere to be seen. I dareswear, my lady, Lord Wylde is not the prince you've painted him as being. He is as heartless as rumored, and—"

"My lord," Lissa cut in, voice crisp and stinging, "that is altogether *enough."*

Langford was past listening, however. "I've detested the

fact that you have been near Wylde these past many days, my lady. No one of your sweet disposition should be so swayed by that monster. The man is an uncouth beast, not fit for your gentle company." Langford snapped his team to an even faster pace, whisking past Gabriel's gates.

"Sir," Lissa demanded, "you will turn this carriage about and take us onto Lord Wylde's property, and you will do so this instant."

Langford shook his head, a sudden, wild gleam in his eyes. "No. Do not try to dissuade me, my lady. I shall not leave you pray to that man's machinations. I am what is best for you, make no mistake. In fact, what I wished to show you on the drive is what is truly in my heart . . . I wished to make you see the light of day."

Harry, listening to their exchange, sat up straighter in the cushions, glancing at Lissa and then Langford, then back at Lissa. His eyes were wide, but not with fright—not yet, anyway. He seemed to be saying to Lissa that Langford was as mad as he'd suggested.

"Wylde will not love you like I will love you," Langford continued. "He cannot, for his heart turned to stone years ago. I cannot abide watching you leave your heart clear for such a swine. I must do what I must do, my lady."

Lissa wrapped her left arm about Harry, pulling the boy closer to her and away from Langford. "And what, pray tell, is that?" she demanded.

"Make you see the truth. I must take charge of this impossible situation you've wound yourself into with Wylde and do what is best . . . for you and for me."

Lissa felt the pounding of pure dread wash through her. She held tighter to Harry. "And the boy?" Lissa asked.

Langford glared down at Harry, who looked quite prepared to stick his tongue out at the man. "He will have to join us, I am afraid," said Langford, turning his attentions back to the road and the bend his team was rounding at a dangerous speed. His top hat was torn away by the wind, leaving his blond hair to be whipped about his head in a crazed manner. Everything about the man appeared crazed. "I cannot chance moving onto Wylde's lands lest you be so foolish as to try and get away, my lady."

Lissa couldn't believe what was happening, what she was hearing. Her own bonnet was in danger of being snatched by the wind, the long ends of its ribbons snapping behind her head. The rush of air smarted her cheeks.

"Stop the carriage, Langford," she demanded. "Stop. *Now.*"

Langford shook his head, hunkered down and drove his team to an even more chaotic pace. Lissa feared they would all meet their deaths, this hideous ride ending in a sickening heap of wheels and horses' hooves.

Langford navigated an especially nasty turn, one that nearly upset the conveyance. The three of them were threatened with a hideous pitch to the right, which nearly promised to see them tossed off the seat and into the ditch alongside the road.

Lissa clutched at Harry to get a firm hold on him. The carriage settled once more onto the roadway, but Langford did not let up on the leathers.

"Your foolish liaison with Wylde was bad enough," he said through clenched teeth, forcing his team onward, "but now you are cozying to the boy Wylde calls his own. I won't have it, Lissa. I will not! I know now I must save you from your own self. In time I know you will come to understand my actions."

"*What* actions?" Lissa cried, alternately watching both the road ahead and Langford and holding close to Harry all the while. "What are you *talking* about?"

"Us. Being together. Forever. I've purchased a special license, my dear. The two of us can soon be married— without fuss, without preamble."

"You *are* mad," Lissa gasped.

"I am not crazed," Langford muttered, "not by far. I *have,* however, seen the light. You are enamored of Wylde, my lady. You have been since the beginning of the Summer

Season. I do not fault you for that. I fault only Wylde for
charming you into something so vile as a liaison—one he
would ultimately end, leaving you with all the shameful
repercussions." He made a deep guttural sound, much
like an animal growl. "Wylde always did have a way with
females," he added, "could make them feel that he was
all they needed, was the only man they could trust. Damme,
but how I detest Wylde and all he is."

Langford was past sanity, Lissa realized. And his horses—
dear God!—he was moving them too fast along the narrow
roadway.

"Take Harry and me back to my home, Langford," Lissa
said.

"I can't do that. I won't."

Lissa felt her stomach turn over. Had she been alone
with Lord Langford in the carriage she might have dared
to throw herself out, onto the ground, leaving herself to
a bone-crushing fate. But she wasn't alone. She had Harry's
safety to consider.

She looked down at Harry. Surprisingly enough, the boy
winked. He obviously had a plot afoot in that fertile, six-
year-old mind of his.

Lissa shook her head, brows furrowing, warning Harry
not to do anything foolish.

Just as Langford neared his team to a spot in the road
that ran adjacent to Gabriel's river lodge, Harry shot to
his feet, leaned against Langford, and let out a hideous
wail.

"What the blazes—?" yelled Langford.

"Ooooh," moaned Harry, clutching with his free arm
at his stomach. He wailed again. "I—I'm going to be ill
. . . lest you stop this carriage, m'lord."

"Sit down!" Langford yelled.

"Can't," said Harry. "Ohhh, but I feel those kippers I
ate coming back up. Here they come, ohhh—"

Langford pulled at the leathers, eventually hauling the
chestnuts to a halt.

"Christ's nails!" he muttered, jumping down and pulling Harry with him, "be sick in the weeds, will you, boy?"

Harry was thrust forward by Langford with unnecessary force, but caught his footing fast enough.

Lissa, realizing that Harry was merely playacting and thus offering the two of them a means of escape, quickly jumped down off the seat from the opposite side. Her muslin caught at the side of the carriage. She yanked the material free with a savage thrust, then rounded the back of the carriage and hurried to Harry's side, catching his left hand up in her right.

"Can you stand, Harry?" she asked loud enough for Langford to hear.

"Ohhh," groaned the boy, pressing against her skirts.

Lissa did not miss his wink as he dared a glance up at her. "At the count of three?" he whispered. "We shall make a run for it, yes?"

Feeling her heart in her throat at his bold, chivalrous and purely selfless act, Lissa gave a quick nod.

Harry made a motion of keeling forward, pretended to begin to retch, and then, fast as he could, he darted away, Lissa following suit.

"NO!" cried Langford. "Lissa, do not do this! Come back!"

But Lissa wasn't listening. Hand in hand with Harry, she scurried to the opposite side of the road, then dashed into the rough woodland.

Too many brambles caught at her skirts, hands and face, and tugged at her hair. She kept going, though. She knew they mustn't stop. If she'd read Harry's mind correctly—which she guessed that she *had*—they were headed for Gabriel's river lodge. Mayhap Harry knew something she did not and was now threading the two of them toward the safe haven of Gabriel's protection. Perhaps Gabriel would be in the lodge and would deal with Langford.

Lissa prayed it was so.

Chapter 17

The going became treacherous as Harry and Lissa neared the river lodge. The foliage thickened, becoming more cumbersome, the ground proving more uneven. Harry's mad dash did not let up, though, and neither did Lissa's.

Her skirts were torn, threaded with prickers and needles, her face scratched for the second time that day. But she kept running. Harry, like a deer, harbored the agility to jump over every fallen branch, to sidestep and swerve around the most nettlesome brambles. The boy seemed to have a sixth sense as to where to lead or not lead, and Lissa blindly followed.

"Lisha," he called, "are you all right?"

"I'm fine, sweetheart. Keep running!"

Like one of Wellington's finest soldiers, he guided them through the thick forest to the door of the lodge, then banged the thing open with a lift of the latch and a hearty push with his shoulders. He blasted inside the place, Lissa hot on his heels.

"Gabriel!" she called out, unable to help herself. "Gabriel, are you here?"

They stumbled inside to silence.

No Gabriel.

No help in the form of a white knight who might bring their dreaded follower to his knees.

Harry, looking frightened for the first time that day, said, "Papa meant to come here, Lisha, I promise! He told me so himself. He came upstairs to tuck me in for a nap. Said he was going to meet you today. At the river lodge. That's why I sneaked away when Miss Fabersham weren't . . . *wasn't* looking."

Harry moved deeper inside the lodge, clearly wishing he could conjure up his father.

Of course! Lissa thought. Gabriel had doubtless sent word to her and had asked for her to meet him at his river lodge! Mayhap even his note was arriving at Clivedon Manor this moment. Where else should their private meeting take place than the spot where he'd first kissed her?

Lissa slammed the door shut, her mind reeling. "Perhaps your papa shall be along shortly," she said, breathless from their mad dash through the woods, and hoping she was correct in thinking Gabriel was on his way.

She was just about to bolt the door when Langford banged it open. The whole of her body was vaulted backward. Lissa fell, her gloved hands scraping hard against the wood floor.

"Get out," she gasped, scurrying backward. "Leave us!"

"Lissa," said Langford, his eyes bright, his mind gone totally mad, "you do not know what you are saying. I have come to help you, not harm you."

"You are frightening to me. And to Harry as well. Leave us, Langford. I want *nothing* to do with you."

"Ahh, Lissa, my lovely Lady Lissa, you do not mean the words you speak."

"I mean them, Langford, more than you'll ever know."

She moved back, felt the leg of the table, then hauled herself upward as she grasped onto that leg.

Langford moved inexorably nearer. "I want only for us to wed. For the two of us to spend the rest of our lives together. You want it, too, Lissa. Admit it. You know you do."

"I want *nothing* to do with you!" Lissa cried. "Nothing, do you *hear*?"

The man seemed to hear nothing, to know nothing other than the want that flamed in his addled brain. "Enough toying with my emotions, my lady. All through the Season you kept my locket in your possession. What was I to think, eh? That you merely enjoyed wearing the piece? That you liked keeping it beneath your pillow, perhaps?"

"I never *kept* the thing . . . it was only lost to me. Had I held it in my possession the afternoon after you pressed it upon me, I would have given it back to you!"

"You expect me to believe that? 'Tis Wylde who has twisted your mind against me. He has confused you, has caused you to think I am wrong for you."

"No!" Lissa shouted. "I have fashioned that fact for myself. The only pity is I did not come to the full realization sooner! Begone, I say!"

Langford pressed closer still. "Wylde isn't the man for you. He never was . . . never could be. Come, Lissa, make the best choice. Be with me."

"Never! 'Tis Lord Wylde's suit I wish for, not yours. Never, ever yours!"

Langford, sleek as a cat, suddenly vaulted against her body with such force that Lissa cried out.

Harry cried out, too. "Let her go!" he screamed. "Let my Lisha go!"

Just then, there came a shadow in the doorway.

"Papa!" Harry yelled.

Langford whipped his gaze about. *"Wylde."*

"Aye, 'tis me. Your worst nightmare come to life."

Gabriel, with his angling rod in one hand, stood in the doorway, a blaze of sunlight outlining his form and casting his face in shadow.

Langford sucked in an audible hiss of a gasp, whirling both himself and Lissa around. His right arm snaked about her throat, holding tightly.

"Unhand the lady, if you please," said Wylde, rather chattily, as though he'd not just entered his lodge and found his son and Lissa held in the throes of a madman.

"If I do not?" challenged Langford, closing his arm more tightly about Lissa's throat.

Harry, charging out from behind the table, raced in front of Langford. "If you do not," he cried, "then my papa will cut you down with his sword . . . or—or he'll challenge you to a duel at dawn! And *you*, sir, shall be no more than a black memory!" As if to punctuate his words, Harry sent one booted toe sharply against Langford's left shin.

Langford reacted by lessening his hold, and Lissa, seizing the moment, yanked away from the man, reaching out for young Harry as she did so.

But Langford was quicker, so angry was he. He lunged for Harry, scooped the boy up into his hold, then moved to the side of the room.

"Langford, no!" Lissa shouted.

Langford, his gaze on Gabriel, sneered. *"Now* what will you do, Wylde, now that I have your . . . *son?"*

"Damn you, Langford," Gabriel said lowly.

Lissa realized that this moment between the men had nothing to do with her really, and everything to do with the age-old animosity between Gabriel and Langford. She looked at Harry, caught up in Langford's arms, and knew the boy was afraid. And with good reason. Until now, Langford had never had total hold of him.

"Let him go," Lissa begged.

But Langford's crazed attention was centered solely on Gabriel now. "I've always hated you, Wylde. Even when we were at University together . . . I hated that your family name back then was more revered than my own, that the coffers you were destined to inherit were far deeper than the ones I would one day claim. I loathed that you could ride better, shoot better, and were more in demand with the ladies."

"Is that why you wooed Jenny?" Gabriel asked.

"Partly. Mostly, actually. I'd thought, at first, that her father was a very rich man. But then I learned of the man's sickness with gambling. The family was near ruin. *That* was the reason they were so eager to marry off their only child, the light of their eyes. And you, ever the gallant, were stupidly willing to erase their debts and marry their daughter."

Gabriel's jaw clenched. "Jenny was indeed the brightest spot in their lives."

"Yes, and you'd have married the lightskirt whether she was rich or penniless, true to you or not. You were ever the white knight where your precious Jenny was concerned."

"She was my close friend," Gabriel said. "My dearest friend."

"Ah, but she wasn't true to you, not in the end. With but a few pretty phrases and small gifts, I soon had her looking fully my way—and I *did* have my way with her, Wylde, many times. That first time with her, I was very surprised to find that you *hadn't* partaken of what she was so willing to give."

Gabriel looked as though he would like to snap Langford's neck in half with his bare hands. "She was in love with you, Langford. She thought you loved her as well and would marry her. She believed in your lies."

"Not so worldly was she, our Jenny? Though a man would have been hard-pressed to think otherwise when she was flirting with him . . ."

"Jenny was a lady, Langford," Gabriel said very lowly. "Never say otherwise. The very temperament that led her father every night to the gaming tables was the same that drew Jenny to men like you. I believe it was something she inherited from him, a restlessness she knew not how to control. Damn you for taking advantage of her one weakness.''

"There you go again," sneered Langford, "ever charging to Jenny's rescue. I am amazed you would do so in front of yet another lady, one you have followed too closely these past many days." Langford nodded toward Lissa. "Is not the likeness amazing, Wylde? I thought the same when I first met her." Langford turned his attention to Lissa. "Forgive me, my lady. You must be totally confused by our conversation about a woman long dead.''

"I am not confused at all," Lissa said. "In fact, a good many things are becoming quite clear to me.''

"Do you know you could be Jenny's twin?" Langford asked. "You've her fair coloring, her eye color . . . even the way you smile is reminiscent of her.''

"Is that why you sought my hand?" Lissa asked. "Because I reminded you of someone you treated most shabbily?''

"It was not *me* who left the lady alone at the altar, to cry in the face of all her guests," Langford said violently. " 'Twas Wylde who did the deed!''

"Only because Jenny asked that I extricate her from her promise of marriage with me," Gabriel said. "She came to me the night before what was to have been our wedding day. She told me she'd fallen in love with another man . . . and that she was carrying his seed. But she knew her parents wanted her to marry me, that she would break their hearts if they thought she'd turned her back on their desires for her and their chance to settle all their many debts. . . . So she asked me, *as her dearest friend,* to try and help extricate her from the web she'd created. I told her I would do what I must to see that her good name was not tarnished, would offer her a way out so that she could go to her lover and eventually marry him instead. I had no idea that *you* were that man, Langford. Not then.''

"Ah, so you played the noble savior, leaving your love

alone at the altar, and allowing Society to believe you were
a beast of a man. How you must have rued that decision
when Jenny's *loving* parents soon sent her away, to the
north of England.''

"Damn you, Langford, they sent her away because of
what you caused to grow within her, and you know it! You
know, too, that she wrote endless letters to you, begging
for you to come and claim her and to be with her on the
day that drew ever nearer. And when that day came, and
her parents fostered out the very creation of her love for
you, you *still* did not go to her. And so she cut her own
wrists rather than live without you and the shame you thrust
upon her. You've her blood on your hands, Langford, not
me.''

Lissa looked at Gabriel, her heart in her eyes. So *this*
was the true tale behind all the rumors about him . . . *this*
was how he'd earned the label of the Heartless Lord Wylde.
No wonder he'd become a recluse, wanting nothing more
to do with people who thought him a fiend. And Harry
. . . dearest God, she thought, *Harry was the product of Jenny's
love for Langford!* Harry was the child Jenny had borne and
then her parents fostered out. Doubtless, Gabriel had gone
in search of the infant, had found him, then brought him
to live alongside the Dove.

Lissa felt a wave of strong, pure emotion wash over her.
How very true and pure and good Gabriel was—and to
think she'd doubted him at times. Never, ever would she
doubt him again!

She whipped her attention to Langford. "Let the boy
go,'' she said, her voice holding a warning tone. "Do it.
Now.''

"Not just yet, I'm afraid. I need a safe exit back to my
carriage. His presence will assure me of that.''

"You are beneath contempt, Langford.''

"And you, my lady, are a perfect fool for choosing Wylde
and his brat over me. We could have had a beautiful future

together. With your fortune and my energies, our life together could have been very sweet indeed.''

"Do not think you will step one foot out of this lodge with my son," Gabriel said.

Harry cried out as Langford savagely yanked him upward in an even tighter hold.

"Move!" Langford yelled to Gabriel. "Or else."

Gabriel moved to one side of the doorway, having no other choice. "I'll get you free, son," he promised as Langford moved past them.

Harry gulped, then smiled nervously.

Langford gripped the boy tighter. "Do not assume to overtake me, Wylde. If you do, I'll make the boy pay for your foolishness."

As Langford was talking, he was also moving to the doorway. Lissa saw Harry send her a wink over Langford's shoulder, trying to tell her with that small sign that he had not run out of ideas. As soon as Langford got to the doorway, Harry wriggled in the man's tight hold, managed to set himself sideways, then flung out both his arms and his legs to the side. His small hands grabbed hold of the door jamb on one side, his toes finding a sturdy latch at the other side. "Hook him, Papa!" Harry shouted.

Gabriel lifted his angling pole, then sent a perfect cast directly at the back of Langford's head. His huge hook— the very same he'd used to catch Lissa's trout the night before—sank into the skin at the back of Langford's head. Gabriel expertly lifted his angling rod, setting the hook deep.

Langford let out a howl, instinctively letting the boy go and reaching to snatch the offensive hook from his head.

Harry managed to right himself as he fell, landed on his rump, then scooted to his feet, dashing back, directly into Lissa's open arms.

"Oh, Harry," she cried, enfolding him in a warm hug.

"I'm okay, Lisha. Truly."

Gabriel, seeing his son safely with Lissa, wound in his

line as he walked toward Langford. He pushed the man out of the lodge, not caring that a yelping Langford stumbled down onto the flagstones.

"Get it out!" Langford begged. "You've pierced my brain, I swear! I'll go to the constable about this, do you hear?"

"I hope you do," Gabriel growled. "In fact, I'll lead you there, with my line. How's that sound? Or perhaps I'll just make fish feed of you, dumping you into the Dove to be gone forever."

"Oh, God," Langford wailed. He dropped to his knees beside the wildflowers outside the stoop, yanking at the offensive hook, but the more he tugged at it, the deeper it embedded itself in his skull. *"Take it out,"* he begged again, more pathetically this time.

"Can't," said Gabriel. "You'll need a surgeon to do the deed. That's the interesting thing about a fish hook, Langford. You have to push it in deeper before you can pull it out. They're troublesome things, these hooks are. And the one I stuck in you is mighty big; sturdy and well-made, too. My guess is it will have to be cut out."

Langford let out a long wail. "Damn you, Wylde!" he cried. "Can you have no pity on me? You've obviously won the lady's heart, and you've that baggage of a boy to boot. Just cut your line and let me go."

Gabriel walked around Langford, then knelt in front of him. "Only on a few conditions," he said, glaring into the man's face that was contorted with pain.

"Anything!" cried Langford, becoming a quivering mass.

"That you leave this shire and never show your face to me again."

"Yes! I'll do it now. This day. I swear it! Just let me go."

"I'm not finished yet, Langford. Should I ever hear of you pursuing another female for reasons other than love, God's truth I will hunt you down and make you pay for what you did to Jenny. I've blunt enough and the daring to do it, Langford, you know I do."

"Yes, yes, I know. I believe you. Just cut me free. I'll never return to Derbyshire. I swear it. And I—I am sorry about Jenny. I am. Whether you believe it or not, I never wanted her to do what she did."

"Save your breath, Langford. I don't even want to hear you utter her name. And I never, ever want you anywhere near Lissa or my son again. Mark my words. The vows I make, I keep—and I vow now that I will kill you should you ever attempt to harm my son or my future wife."

Langford swallowed convulsively, nodding, his eyes wide with fear. "I hear you. I believe you. Go. Go back inside with your Lissa and your boy, just please let me be," Langford cried.

Gabriel got to his feet. He drew out his pocket knife, cut the line with a final act, then pushed Langford away from him.

Langford scrambled to his feet, the hook still impaled in his head, and then he ran fast into the woods, heading for his carriage and a hasty flight away from the man he knew he could never best.

Wylde watched him go, then went inside the lodge.

Lissa was sitting on the bench of the worktable, Harry on her lap. She was talking quietly with the boy, soothing away any of the fears still within him.

"Is he gone?" she asked.

"For good," he answered. "I believe the two of us finally came to an understanding. He will never bother you or Harry again. In fact, I do believe he'll never dare to return to our shire."

Lissa glanced up at Gabriel. *"Our* shire?"

Gabriel nodded. "You heard me aright." Looking at her, he felt his heart turn over. "What a beautiful sight," he murmured, "to see my son in the arms of the woman I hope will soon become his mother and my wife."

Lissa caught her bottom lip between her teeth . . . and then she smiled, tears gathering in her eyes. "Do you mean that, Gabriel?"

"Aye," he said softly, sincerely. "With all my heart and soul."

Lissa visibly trembled, then glanced down at Harry. "What do you think of that idea, Harry? Would you like your papa and you and me to become a family?"

Harry straightened, then threw his arms about her neck. "Oh, yesh, Lisha!" he said, thoroughly slurring all of his *S*'s.

Lissa laughed and hugged him in return. "Then I guess it shall be a pact between the three of us. But I must warn you, Harry—and Gabriel, you, too—that a pact made near the Dove lasts a lifetime. My father once told me so. Like the river, these pacts are strong and deep and ever flowing. Indeed, they are neverending."

Gabriel came around the bench, straddled the thing by throwing one leg over it, then settled down beside Lissa and his son, his thighs pressing against Lissa's body. " 'Tis the kind of pact I know best," he murmured, placing a kiss on her temple, then smoothing one hand over her hair that had been whipped about by her mad carriage ride and even madder dash to the lodge.

He then ran his hand along his son's cheek, smiling at the boy. "What's your opinion, Harry? Should we welcome Lissa into our family, move her things across the Dove— or mayhap move *our* things across the river?"

"I don't care what we move or where," said Harry. "I just want Lisha for my mama and for the three of us to be happy."

Gabriel laughed.

Lissa laughed, too.

Gabriel suddenly nuzzled his face against hers. "You had something to say to me, my sweet, some matter of import to discuss?"

"So you *did* come here to meet me," she said.

"Aye, that I did. I would walk to the ends of the world for you, Lissa, and beyond. Never doubt that."

"I won't," she whispered, pressing her face against his, loving the feel of him, the scent of him. "What I wanted to tell you today is that . . . that I'd come to the conclusion that I *am* in the mind of marrying—but that I wish to marry only you."

"So Langford never had a prayer?"

Lissa frowned at mention of the man's name. *"Never.* It's only been you, Gabriel."

"Ah, there, you've said it again; said my name. How I love the sound of my Christian name passing your lips. *I love you, Lissa."*

"Oh, Gabriel," she breathed, hugging Harry tightly even as she melted against the man she'd come to love more than anything. "I love you, too. I think I have felt this way since the first time I viewed you at the river's edge . . ."

Gabriel kissed her eyes, her nose, her mouth. Harry giggled. Gabriel opened one eye, looking down at his son. "Is this the secret you shared with Lissa while in the tree?"

Harry nodded. "The very one," he said.

"Hmmm . . . I thought so."

Gabriel kissed Lissa again, as Harry, seemingly over the many ordeals of the day, wriggled out of Lissa's lap, then scurried away, gathering up three of the long poles that were housed on the opposite wall.

"I do believe our son wishes to fish, m'lord."

"Gabriel," he growled against her lips.

"Gabriel," she murmured, her mouth forming a smile even as he kissed it again and again and again.

Long seconds later, Gabriel lifted his face, looked longingly into Lissa's eyes and said, "Do you know what tomorrow is?"

"A new beginning for the three of us?" she ventured.

"Aye. It is that. And it is also Sunday. What say you that

our family heads to the church and finds our own special
boxed pew? I should like to pray again, Lissa, and to offer
up thanks for the fact that you and Harry are with me,
that we've found our way to being a family.''

"Oh, Gabriel,'' she murmured, emotion choking her,
unable to say more.

It was enough. His heart, at last, was full. Life along the
Dove would be everything he'd ever dreamt about, with
Lissa and Harry, and the many other children he and Lissa
would create.

"We shall have the most beautiful life together, Lissa,''
he promised. "We'll begin every day in each other's arms,
and end each day in the same. In between we shall worry
over our children and love them, and teach them about
flies, and trout, and angling, and about the wonders found
alongside the Dove.''

"Children? As in many of them?'' Lissa teased.

"As many as you are willing to create with me, my sweet,''
said Gabriel sincerely.

Lissa felt wonderfully warm inside. "We shall have as
many as we have,'' she said, trusting now in the future.
"And Harry shall make a famous older brother—or a perfect only child. Whatever our future holds, Gabriel, I wish
to share it with you and Harry. Forever. For always.''

Gabriel squeezed her tight. "Mayhap I shall write the
definitive book about night angling for trout.''

"How perfectly wonderful. And I shall make the sketches
for your book, yes?''

"Yes,'' he said, kissing her again. Always he would kiss
her, he knew, for Lissa was his soul mate, the life partner
he'd been lacking.

Much later, Lissa and Gabriel got up off the bench,
then moved to join their son in preparing for a busy day
alongside the river.

Finally," said Harry, grinning. "I'd thought you had forgotten me."

"Never that!" both Lissa and Gabriel said in perfect unison.

Together, the three of them headed out of the lodge, toward the river, and into a bright, sun-filled future.